Ghosts of Coronado Bay

A MAYA BLAIR
MYSTERY

BY

JG FAHERTY

JournalStone

San Francisco

JournalStone books may be ordered through booksellers or by contacting:

JournalStone
199 State Street
San Mateo, CA 94401
www.journalstone.com

ISBN: 978-1-936564-09-5 (sc)
ISBN: 978-1-936564-10-1 (ebook)

Library of Congress Control Number: 2011930595

Printed in the United States of America

JournalStone rev. date: June 10, 2011

Cover Design: Denise Daniel
Cover Art: Philip Renne

Edited by: Edwina Jackson

Acknowledgements

Writing a book is hard work; don't ever let anyone tell you differently. You spend months at the computer, not only writing but rewriting. And proofreading. And emailing people. At times your eyes want to fall out of your head, your back feels permanently bent into unnatural shapes, and you imagine you're turning into a blob of jelly no matter how often you get up to stretch your legs (which often leads to visiting the refrigerator!). But somehow it all seems worth it when you see those hours of work transformed into something you can hold, a book with pages and a cover that is ready to be shared with the world.

It's also true that you can't do it alone. And, for that I say "thank you," as always, to my wife Andrea, who accepts the time I spend in my office even if she can't understand how I can drag myself out of bed so early on Saturday and Sunday mornings when I could be sleeping. She doesn't understand the "need" to write, but she is still my best salesperson and promoter, better at talking about me than I am about myself.

Thanks also to my usual suspects, those people who lend second pairs of eyes, professional advice, or plain old encouragement: Michael McBride, Shaun Jeffrey, Stephen Owen, Hank Schwaeble, Greg Lamberson, Rick Hautula, Kathy Ptacek, Dave Simms, Thomas F. Monteleone, Lee Thomas, Jeff Strand, and Benjamin Kane. Very special thanks also to Jeff Mariotte and John Passarella for the early readings.

To Christopher Payne, thanks for taking a chance on this book and for having the vision to see it in print even before I did.

To all my friends - you know who you are! - thanks so much for your support and for spreading the word on Facebook, Twitter, and all sorts of other places.

To my Mom and Dad - as always, thank you for being my very first readers back when I wrote in pencil and thought writing was so easy anyone could do it.

Finally, a big thank you to all the people who read my books and stories. It's because of you that writers get to write. Keep buying our books - whether written on paper or stored electronically - so we can keep entertaining you.

If I've forgotten anyone, I apologize. There's never enough room to thank everyone you need to. Just remind me, and I'll make sure you get into the next one.

Last but not least, to Harley and Buffy for getting me away from the desk so I can walk you, feed you, and sometimes just sit on the floor with you - thanks!

Prelude

Coronado Bay, 1908

The storm came out of nowhere, lashing the Black Lady with forty-mile-per-hour winds and rain that hit hard enough to leave red welts on exposed flesh. Captain Jonas Freeman shouted for his crew to pile more coal into the furnaces as he struggled with the wheel, fighting to keep the small ship aimed towards the relative safety of the coast.

Freeman swore at the weather, and his own foolish greed, as another gust of gale-force wind pushed the Black Lady farther out to sea. Under normal circumstances a river steamer such as his would never be out in open water to begin with, but the lure of Gavin Hamlin's gold had been too strong.

"It's only a few hours up the coast," the dapper young man had said, his cultured voice at once cajoling and filled with hidden danger. "Surely the Black Lady can handle some waves?"

Damn that evil-hearted dandy! Now they'd be lucky to make it to shore alive, let alone with the boat in one piece.

As if summoned by Freeman's angry thoughts, Gavin Hamlin appeared in the doorway, his shoulder-length black hair tangled and soaked from wind, rain, and sea spray, his long fingers gripping the door frame so tightly their knuckles looked like snow caps atop flesh-colored mountains. As always, his face held the same sickly-pale hue of a hospital patient.

But his eyes were still as black and deep as bottomless pits.

"Captain! How far from Boston are we?"

"Boston?" Freeman couldn't believe the man's one-track mind. "An eternity, if we don't find a shelter of some kind, be it cove or island. This storm'll smash us apart like a toy."

"What chance if we continue forward, that the storm will fall behind us?"

Freeman shook his head, wondering who the bigger idiot was, he for accepting Hamlin's offer, or Hamlin for not understanding the basics of New England weather despite living in the region all his life.

"None. Wind's blowing west to east, pushing us farther to sea. Storm like this one'll hang on for hours, maybe into the 'morrow."

"Damn it to Hell. All right, do what you can. But the moment the weather lets up, we continue north."

The tall man, hardly out of boyhood, disappeared before Freeman could reply, turning sideways so Benson, the first mate, could enter the cabin.

"I found a map!" Water dripped from Benson's soaked jacket as he spread a crumpled piece of paper on the desk. Once opened, it showed a surprisingly detailed map of the New England coastline. Considering the Black Lady had never been farther out to sea than the mouth of the Hudson River, Freeman thought it a wonder they even had any maps of the coast on board.

Maybe Lady Luck is with us after all.

"Captain, there's an island not too far ahead if we stay on our present heading. It's right on the border between Rhode Island and Massachusetts, twelve miles off shore."

"Aye, and naturally so small we'll be lucky as all get-out to find it in this mess," Freeman said, looking at where Benson's finger pointed. "But it's the closest thing to us, and our engines aren't strong enough to fight these damned winds. Full speed ahead, Mister Benson."

"Aye, sir." Benson hurried from the cabin.

Freeman stared out at the gale and tightened his grip on the wheel until his hands felt as if they might freeze there forever.

Half an hour. That's all I ask, Lord. Just keep us together another half hour, and I swear I'll never gamble or go whoring again.

He was still praying when the Black Lady struck one of the many rocky shoals surrounding Coronado Island.

As icy water filled his lungs and the screams of drowning men echoed through in his head, one final thought played over and over in his brain.

I wish I'd never met Gavin Hamlin. May his soul rot in Hell forever.

In the dark depths of the ocean, the Black Lady settled to the bottom in a cloud of silt and muck. The fish and lobsters, the only living witnesses, hurried out of its way.

In the eternal blackness, the spirits of the dead howled with grief and anger.

All except two.

Chapter 1

Coronado Island, Present Day

The late afternoon sun gilded the tops of the waves in gold as Maya Blair walked the wide, mostly empty sidewalk of Coronado Bay's Main Street. It was almost five, a time when the majority of residents were either making dinner or eating it.

Approaching the Bay Diner, Maya gave a low groan as she saw the parking area filled to overflowing, indicating yet another busy dinner shift. For the billionth time, she wished her parents hadn't decided to give up their regular jobs and buy the diner five years ago. Not that she begrudged their following their dream, but their owning the diner meant she had to work there too, and waiting tables most certainly wasn't *her* dream.

Of course, the odds were pretty good that even if they hadn't owned the diner, she'd have ended up waitressing there or working nights and weekends at the Gap, like her best friend Lucy.

Not like there's a lot of jobs to choose from when you live on a one-town island. At least I don't have to worry about getting fired.

Entering the diner was like entering her second home. The delicious smells of her mother's homemade recipes mixed well with the standard odors of coffee, hot grease, and frying hamburgers. Swirled and tossed around by the overhead fans, the rich, homey goodness twisted between the tables and booths, swept past the long counter, and exited through the doors and exhaust system to the outside, where they served as free advertising, beckoning people to come in and stay a while.

Meatloaf, stuffed cabbage, eggplant parmigiana, beef stew. She'd have known what was cooking even if she didn't know the Thursday specials by heart.

"Maya!" her mother's voice came, loud and anxious. "Hurry up and grab an apron! Tessa called in sick again."

Crap. Maya waved a hand to let her mother know she'd heard her, and then ducked into the storage room and pulled a black apron off a rack. Tessa Farr had a habit of calling in sick at the worst times. She always made up the hours, but in the meantime it meant Maya and Jessica, the other full-time waitress, would have to handle the rush themselves.

No sooner had she tied on her apron than her father rang the bell at the kitchen window, indicating another order needed fast delivery. "Order up!"

"Got it," Maya said, grabbing the two plates of eggplant and pasta.

"Table seventeen," Jessica shouted from where she stood by a booth, taking someone's order.

Maya hurried through the obstacle course of tables and chairs and delivered the dinners to two old men. One of them had the local newspaper open on the table, and she caught a glimpse of the headline.

"Museum to Open Black Lady Exhibit on Friday"

She smiled to herself. No need to read *that* article. The Maritime Museum, Coronado Island's only tourist attraction other than a few miles of stony beach and a supposedly haunted lighthouse on the opposite side of the island, was counting on a big opening day turnout for their new exhibit. Maya's history class would be there too, Mrs. Brackenberry having somehow managed to schedule a private tour.

Wonder how the old goat did that? Probably taught the museum's head curator a hundred years ago.

As soon as the words popped into her head, Maya scolded herself for the mean thought. Mrs. Brackenberry was a nice lady and a decent teacher. Just out of touch with the times. Seriously out of touch. Like, she'd need a time machine to get back in touch.

I think some of Lucy's sarcasm is rubbing off on me. Why couldn't it be her self-confidence instead?

While the idea of spending an afternoon staring at pieces of an old boat dredged up from the ocean floor didn't appeal to her in the least, it *would* be nice to get out of school for a couple of hours. At least they didn't have to tour the rest of the museum. Like every other person on the island, Maya knew the place nearly as well as the people who worked there.

Ding! "Order up!"

Maya sighed. Compared to waiting tables, even the museum sounded good.

* * *

By seven o'clock, Maya was sick to death of hearing people talk about the new museum exhibit like it was the greatest discovery since sliced bread.

If I hear one more person say they can't wait to see--

"I'm going first thing in the morning." A woman at a nearby table waved a forkful of meatloaf at the other two people sitting with her. "First thing. I cannot wait to see what they found inside that old ship."

That's it!

"Dad! I'm taking my break." Without waiting for an answer, Maya hurried through the kitchen and out the back door. Inhaling deeply of the warm September air, she leaned against the building and concentrated on her breathing, the way her karate instructor had taught her.

"In and out. Slow and easy. Each time you exhale, release some of your tension. Each time you inhale, picture calmness entering your body."

"Looks like something's got you upset."

Maya opened her eyes and smiled at the unexpected, but always welcome, visitor. "Hi, Grandma. Is it that obvious?"

Elsa Crompton, Maya's maternal grandmother, shook her head, making her gray curls bob like buoys on the water. "Is it that obvious, she asks? A person wouldn't have to know you for sixteen years to see something's troubling you. What's the matter?"

"I dunno." Maya twirled a lock of her own dark auburn - Lucy called it black cherry - hair around two fingers, a habit she'd had since grade school. "I guess I'm just in a bad mood today. All my friends are at the Lanes, and I'm stuck here. Plus I've got a ton of homework I still have to do, and the whole town won't stop babbling about a stupid boat exhibit at the museum."

Elsa patted her granddaughter on the shoulder. "Sounds like you're just being a teen-ager. Hormones, you know. They get all out of sorts at your age, especially when boys are around."

Maya gave a sarcastic laugh. "Boys? Ha. I wish that were a problem."

"What happened to that husky fellow you were dating?"

"Stuart?" Maya shook her head. "He turned out to be a jerk. The kind of guy who thinks he owns you, always has to know where you're going, who you're with, what time you'll be home. I told him we were through." Just thinking of Stuart Newman made her scowl.

"And how did he take that?"

"Exactly the way I figured he would. He accused me of cheating on him and said if he saw me with another guy, there'd be trouble."

"Stay away from him, dear. He sounds dangerous."

"You don't have to tell me twice. I plan on avoiding him like a convenience store burrito."

Elsa chuckled, and then her face grew serious. "Speaking of danger, I've been having bad feelings lately, like something is wrong in Coronado Bay."

"Is that like when Mom has a bad dream and then tells me I shouldn't go to the beach?"

"Just be careful, all right?"

Maya leaned up and kissed her grandmother on the cheek. "Sure thing. Thanks for stopping by and cheering me up. I know how hard it is for you to come here."

"Anything for you, dear. Have a good night." Elsa smiled once more and then faded from sight.

Feeling better, Maya opened the door and went back inside. Her grandmother's visits always cheered her up. She wished the rest of the family could still talk to Grandma Elsa, but the knack for seeing and speaking to ghosts - and, in Maya's case, making them temporarily solid by being near them - had passed from Elsa to Maya, skipping Maya's mother in the process. Grandma Elsa said it had as much to do with belief as natural ability, one of the reasons Elsa had made Maya promise to keep the secret of her ability to herself, even from her parents.

"Most people don't want to know ghosts are real. It would just make them sad or scared."

Not that there were a lot of ghosts to talk to or even see. Counting her grandmother, Maya knew of exactly one. Grandma Elsa said there were others, but they weren't as common as people thought.

"Only rarely does a person's spirit stay on after they die," Elsa said one time, back when Maya was only seven or eight and talking to a dead person still seemed so amazing. "Usually it's when a person is taken before they're ready to go, and even then the person has to be very strong-willed."

"Mommy told me I'm the most stubborn person she's ever met," Maya had replied. "Does that mean I'd make a good ghost?"

Elsa had laughed out loud at her granddaughter's question. "You'd make a great ghost, my dearest. One of the best."

One of the reasons Maya appreciated her grandmother's visits so much was because she knew how hard it was for Elsa to appear in Coronado Bay. She'd died in a car accident in New York, in a taxi on the way to the airport after visiting her brother. While it was apparently easy for ghosts to manifest - a word Maya learned way before her peers - near where they died, it got harder and harder the farther they traveled from their place of death. Grandma Elsa's visits rarely lasted longer than five minutes or so, and even then Elsa often looked fuzzy around the edges by the end.

It was hard to think of something composed of pure energy as getting tired, but it happened. Maya just accepted it and enjoyed the visits as best she could.

Considering the alternative, five minutes a couple times a week isn't so bad. Some of my friends never get to see their grandparents.

Her father's voice crashed through her thoughts like a boat plowing through waves. "Maya! Break time's over. I need a box of rolls and more coleslaw!"

Maya allowed herself a small groan and headed for the pantry. *Rolls and coleslaw. Will the excitement never end?*

* * *

The rest of the night stayed just as hectic as the first two hours of Maya's shift. By the time she left the diner at nine to go home and finish her homework, her grandmother's vague warnings of danger were long gone, pushed aside by thoughts of biology, Stuart Newman, and what to wear to school tomorrow.

Chapter 2

Kyle Forster and George Gibson grunted and huffed as they heaved a large coil of rope, thick as a man's wrist, onto a table. They'd spent all of the afternoon, and much of the night, putting the finishing touches on the Black Lady exhibit at Coronado Bay's Maritime Museum. The job was made more difficult than it should have been by the odd disturbances that kept happening, disturbances like the ones that already had the opening a month behind schedule. Dr. Bruce Griffith, who was overseeing the project, had let everyone know in no uncertain terms that he'd accept no more delays.

It was no secret around the museum that since the moment the remnants of the Black Lady arrived, strange things had been happening – lights flickering on and off when people weren't in rooms, boxes falling to the floor when no one stood near them, and tools that never stayed where you left them. And, things only got worse once Griffith's team started putting the exhibit together in the main exhibit room. Each morning, the staff arrived already knowing they'd have to pick up an assortment of display items that had fallen off seemingly level shelves and tables during the night.

After a while, the constant straightening of the previous night's unexplained occurrences started to wear on even the most laid back employees.

Dr. Griffith and most of the museum's senior staff chalked it up to a combination of clumsiness, old wiring, warped shelves, and possibly a small rodent problem. But several of the employees, especially those who worked exclusively on the Black Lady exhibit, had a different theory.

Haunts.

Some said ghosts; others favored poltergeists. A couple even talked about gremlins. But they all agreed something weird was going on, and it hadn't started until they'd opened the crates containing the remains of the Black Lady.

Now, as Kyle and George admired their handiwork, a box of water-stained, illegible documents slid off a nearby shelf and crashed to the floor, startling curses and exclamations from both of them.

"Damn! I hate when that happens," Kyle said, holding a hand to his chest.

"Ol' Griffith would probably say the shelf ain't level." George pointed at the offending piece of wood. "He'd be wrong, though. I measured it twice yesterday, and it's perfect. But that box keeps slidin' off."

Kyle shrugged. "You know what to do."

"Yeah." George took a roll of Velcro tape from his work belt. In order to end the time-consuming process of picking things up over and over, the whole staff had taken to using the tape to stick everything but the heaviest display items in place. Without it, they might never have gotten the exhibit open. Even Dr. Griffith hadn't complained.

"There." George gave the box a test push. It didn't move. "That's the end of it. We're done and outta here."

"And good riddance," Kyle said as they flipped off the lights and let the heavy doors swing shut. "I never want to spend another night here. Damn place gives me the major creeps."

The two men continued complaining as they walked down the hall, their voices gradually fading away until the only sounds in the exhibit room were the soft ticking of a wall clock and the ever-present groans and creaks all old buildings make in the night.

Five minutes after George and Kyle left the building, the ceiling lights flickered on and off several times, creating a strobe effect across the tables and cabinets containing the items salvaged from the rusted hulk of the Black Lady.

A figure emerged from the shadows, a tall, thin figure, moving with silent ease between the crowded displays. Several other men followed him.

"I thought they'd never leave," the tall man said, his youngish face looking older than its years in the dim glow of the room's emergency lights. "Start searching. Once the exhibit opens tomorrow, this place will be crawling with people every day, which means we'll only have nights to look for the key."

An older man, his shoulders hunched from years of manual labor, his pale face leathery and worn by too many years of exposure to harsh weather, shook his head.

"What's the use? Even if we find it, we've no way of unlocking the box and removing the book."

The thin man scowled. "Leave that to me. I'll figure out a way. I'll be damned if I don't get back what's rightfully mine."

The half-dozen figures spread out through the room, peering into cases, looking underneath anchors and hull plates and thick metal chains all pitted and corroded from over a century of lying on the ocean floor.

As the men carried out their relentless search, a seventh figure stood in the shadows of the doorway watching them.

Unlike the others, he prayed they *wouldn't* find what they were looking for.

Because it might mean the end of the world.

* * *

"I don't believe what I'm hearing. You're not going to the dance? You have to go. Everyone will be there."

Maya shook her head at Lucy Patton's incredulous look. "Not me," she told the girl who'd been her best friend since fourth grade. "I am so not going to be the biggest loser in the junior class. I'd rather stay home and watch television with my parents than go to the Homecoming Dance by myself."

"But you won't be alone. At least, not after you walk in. You'll be with me and Gary and everyone."

"Oh, that makes it so much better. Instead of being the third wheel with you and your boy toy, I can be the seventh or ninth wheel with a whole bunch of couples. No thanks."

Any stranger seeing the two girls walking home from school would have been forgiven for mistaking them for sisters. Both were average height and build, with blue eyes and hair down to their shoulders. On closer inspection, however, a person would see that Lucy's hair was closer to strawberry than cherry, and her eyes several shades lighter than Maya's. Lucy was fond of saying they were opposite twins - one dark, one light, one serious, one crazy.

No one that knew them disagreed.

A brisk wind shook the trees as they rounded the corner onto Franklin Street, the long road that paralleled Coronado Bay's Main Street and led from the school to the neighborhoods where Maya and Lucy lived. A few red and yellow leaves, harbingers of the approaching autumn, took flight around them, miniature kites zigging and zagging through the air.

With her usual pitbull stubbornness, Lucy continued her attempt to change Maya's mind. "You know, you could have had a date. All you had to do was wait until *after* the dance to dump Stuart."

"Yeah, right. Put up with more of his crap just so I could go to a dance with a guy who's suddenly decided that girls are supposed to be docile little slaves who do whatever their boyfriends say? What drugs are you taking? I want some."

"Very funny. Ha, ha, you should be on *America's Got Talent*. I'm serious. I want you there with us. It won't be the same without you."

"Well, unless someone decides to take pity on the ugly duckling with the psychotically jealous ex-boyfriend, methinks I'll be spending Homecoming in my room with a bottle of diet Coke, watching bad Tori Spelling movies on *Lifetime*."

They reached the corner of Dunes Lane where Lucy lived. "Well, I've got a week to change your mind. That's *my* mission."

Maya laughed. "Don't quit your day job. I'll call you after dinner."

"Later."

Maya waved goodbye and continued walking. She still had two blocks to go before Beach Street, where her parents owned a two-story Cape Cod that seemed to get smaller and more crowded each year, even with her brother Joe away at college.

"Maya, we need to talk."

The voice from behind startled her, even as she recognized it. She turned around and confronted the husky boy stepping out from the obscurity of a large tree.

"Stuart. I already told you. We have nothing to talk about. And, why are you following me like some kind of creepy stalker?"

Stuart Newman spread his hands. "'Cause waiting for you here was the only way I could get you alone. All I'm asking is five minutes."

Having dated Stuart for three months, Maya knew how stubborn he was, and that sooner or later she'd have to deal with the confrontation she'd been avoiding. "Fine. Five minutes. Start talking."

"What, here?" He frowned, his thick eyebrows dipping down until they nearly met in the middle, creating a giant, hairy caterpillar across his forehead. "Let's go to your house."

"It's now or never." She tapped her watch. "Time's a-wastin'. I've got a paper to write."

"Okay, okay. Geez, you can be such a bitch. Look, all I want to say is I'm sorry. I don't know what I did to piss you off, but whatever it was, I apologize, okay? I just want things to be like they were."

Maya took a deep breath before replying. There had to be a way to explain things to him so he'd understand, without causing another shouting match like the last time.

"You don't get it. The way things 'were' is exactly what I *don't* want. You were too possessive and waaay too jealous. That's why it'll never work between us."

Stuart's frown grew harder, and a red glow crept up from his neck and spread across his square face. "You know, a lot of girls would consider it a compliment that their boyfriend wanted to spend time with them."

Maya felt her control slipping. "Spend time with me? You wouldn't give me a chance to breathe by myself! You had to walk me to school, walk me to my classes, eat lunch with me, go to the mall with me, walk me to work. You got pissed off if I wanted to hang out with Lucy; you got pissed when I wouldn't let you come to my karate class and watch me. And, don't try telling my it was 'cause you wanted to be around me. You just wanted to make sure no one else talked to me."

"That's bull. I never said you couldn't talk to people!"

Stuart's voice had grown louder, and Maya found herself shouting back at him. "Oh, yeah? What about the time Chuck Henderson asked if he could borrow my homework, and you threatened to put his head through a locker?"

"Don't bring that up. That's different. It was a guy!"

"See? It's all about jealousy." Maya stopped, closed her eyes, and counted to five. When she felt calmer, she opened her eyes and looked at Stuart. Veins bulged at his temples, his fists were clenched, and a muscle twitched along the side of his jaw. Even though she could tell he wouldn't listen, she made one last attempt at rational conversation.

"Stuart. There're a lot of girls who like the kind of attention you give a girl. I'm just not one of them. You need to find someone who likes you for you. And, I need to find someone who lets me be me."

He stared at her, and for a moment she thought maybe, just maybe, she'd gotten through to him. Then, something changed in his face, as if he'd just learned his homework had been stolen.

"I get it now. There's somebody else, isn't there? If I find out you've been cheating on me--"

"Stuart. Grow the hell up. There's no one else. I just don't want to go out with *you*. Period. I'm sorry, but that's just the way it is."

Maya walked away, hoping he'd finally gotten the message to leave her the hell alone. She'd gone about fifteen feet when he spoke again. This time his words were cold, hard, and mean.

"You'll be sorry, all right, you slut. And, so will any guy I catch you with."

Maya turned around, alarmed at the threatening tone in Stuart's voice, but he was already gone.

"Great. School's gonna be a barrel of laughs tomorrow."

* * *

"I can't believe he actually said that! He called you a slut? *You?*" Even through the tiny speaker of Maya's cell phone, the eager shock in Lucy's voice came through loud and clear. "I know nuns sluttier than you."

"I know, right?" Maya had called Lucy right after dinner to tell her about the scene with Stuart. "He totally freaked on me. I've never seen him so bad."

"Is he doing drugs?"

Maya rolled her eyes. "Stuart? No way. You know him. No drugs, no drinking, no cigarettes. Gotta stay healthy for football."

"Maybe that's why he's so angry."

They both laughed, and then Lucy grew serious.

"What are you gonna do about him?"

"Nothing. What can I do, except stay the heck away?"

"What happens if somebody asks you out? You don't want Stu going Godzilla on some poor guy."

"Yeah, 'cause the guys are really lining up at my door to ask me out. That's one thing I don't have to worry about."

"Cut the Ugly Betty routine, Maya. This ain't ninth grade anymore. You're not fat, you've got a pretty face, and you've finally got boobs. Sooner or later some idiot's gonna ask you out."

"Ha, ha. Easy for you to say, you've dated three guys in the past three months."

"That's what happens when you put out, girl. Guys want to be with you."

"Whatever. I gotta go. I'll see you in school tomorrow."

"Later!"

Maya turned off her phone and opened her textbook. She still had math and biology to finish, and it was already nine o'clock. As usual, she'd spent too much time talking to Lucy.

Another late night. Oh, well. That's why God invented energy drinks.

Still, as hard as she tried, she couldn't concentrate on her math problems. Was Lucy right? Would she have a better chance of finding a decent boyfriend if guys knew she'd have sex with them?

An image came to her, of Stuart naked in her bed. Although she'd never 'knocked boots,' as Lucy liked to say, with Stu, they'd gone far enough for her to regret getting even that physical with him. She could only imagine how much worse his jealousy would be if they'd actually gone all the way.

And, what about the future? Would the next guy be the one, or another douche like Stu?

What if I do it with the wrong guy? I don't want to wait 'til I'm married, but I do want to be in love with the person who's my first, not lose it to someone who ends up being a jerk.

And that was the problem, right there. All the girls she knew didn't care about love. Most went with the three-date rule, and there were more than a few who had no problem hooking up with a guy on the first date, or even without a date. Some didn't even care if they went with a guy or a girl, or both.

Any port in a storm. Another of Lucy's sayings, after a night where she'd had a major hot and heavy with Amy Landhouse.

And, yet, I'm the one who gets called a slut.

Giving up on her homework, Maya turned on the computer. Maybe working on her blog for awhile would get her mind off sex and boys, or her lack of both.

* * *

Two hours later, when she finally turned off the lights and went to bed, she was still as aggravated, horny, and depressed as ever.

Chapter 3

"Hey, Maya, heard Stuart dumped your sorry ass. Maybe I'll ask him to the dance."

Maya looked up from her salad and found Mary Ellen Gordon and three other cheerleaders standing at the end of the lunch table, all of them wearing evilly happy grins.

"Go ahead, ask him. I hope he says yes. You'd be doing me a favor." Maya returned to her sandwich and her conversation with Lucy, purposely acting as if Mary Ellen wasn't there.

"Rumor has it he dumped you 'cause you were sleeping around. But we know that can't be true."

Maya clenched her teeth, but refused to look up. *Don't give her the satisfaction. Don't--*

"After all, everyone knows those legs have a 'do not open' sign in between them."

That does it.

"Better that than the revolving door between your fat thighs, Mary Ellen."

Next to Maya, Lucy snorted laughter and soda onto her tray.

"My thighs are not fat!" Mary Ellen dropped her tray onto the table, causing heads to turn throughout the cafeteria.

Lucy made an exaggerated surprised face. "No, and J-Lo's butt isn't big, either."

Mary Ellen's cheeks turned purple, and she took a step toward Lucy, but the other cheerleaders grabbed her. "Not here," one of them said. "You'll get suspended, and you'll miss the dance."

For a moment, Mary Ellen looked like she might ignore her friend's advice. Lucy stood up, and Maya joined her, hands at her sides but ready, the way she'd learned in karate. Maya counted five breaths, during which time no one moved. Then, Mary Ellen pointed a finger at them.

"This isn't over. I'm gonna kick both your asses when you least expect it."

Maya waited until Mary Ellen picked up her tray and the girls walked off before sitting back down. Immediately, Lucy thumped the table with her hand. "That was sooo cool! I can't believe you actually stood up to her."

Looking at her shaking hands, Maya said, "Yeah. Real cool. Now I've gotta watch out for them *and* Stuart."

"Bull. Mary Ellen's all talk. The last time she had a fight was in fifth grade." Lucy took a sip of her soda, let out a loud burp, and then frowned. "Do you think Stu's the one who made up that story about you banging someone else?"

Maya shrugged. "Him or one of his locker room buddies. If you'd asked me two days ago, I'd have said no way. But, after all the things he said about me yesterday..."

Lucy stood up. "You know what? Screw him. Serves him right to get all bent out of shape thinking that. C'mon, let's get going. We've got our museum trip in a few minutes, and I wanna grab a smoke before we go."

"You go ahead. I'm gonna pee and fix my hair. I'll meet you at the bus."

"Catch you in ten, girl." Lucy walked away.

Maya stared at the remains of her lunch and decided she wasn't hungry anymore. *Damn that Stuart Newman!* Even when he wasn't around, he managed to make her life miserable.

The only consolation was neither Stu nor Mary Ellen would be at the museum, which meant she wouldn't have to deal with either of them until Monday.

Maybe I'll get lucky, and they'll forget about me by then.

She smiled at her own wishful thinking.

Yeah, and maybe I'll meet the man of my dreams in the museum today, too.

* * *

For once, the bathroom was empty when Maya entered. After taking care of business and washing her hands, she brushed her hair and checked her makeup. She was dabbing on lipstick when someone said her name in the empty room.

Turning quickly, she found Grandma Elsa standing by a bathroom stall.

"Grandma! You scared the hell out of me."

"Sorry, dear. I didn't mean to."

"It's just that, well, you don't show up in the mirror, you know?"

Elsa nodded. "Is everything all right? I had a...feeling you were upset."

"Just school sh...er, stuff. Nothing major." Maya returned to the mirror, finished her lipstick, and then added some blush to cover the scattering of freckles on her cheeks and nose.

"Are you sure? I'm still getting a feeling that you're in danger."

Maya turned around and gave her grandmother a smile. "Really, there's nothing to worry about. It's high school, and a lot of people are jerks."

"Well, if you want to talk..."

"Nothing to talk about. At least not today." Maya kissed Elsa on the cheek. "I gotta go. We have a class trip in like two minutes. We can talk over the weekend."

Maya headed for the door, eager to get away before her grandmother could ask any more questions. Lying to a ghost was so much harder than to a real person, especially when that ghost knew you better than anyone else, including your parents.

Two girls came walking in as she opened the door, chatting on their cell phones and with each other.

Just before the door shut behind her, Maya heard their gasps as they watched the figure of the old woman fading away.

Laughing to herself, she hurried down the hall to the main entrance.

* * *

"...And, here we see a perfectly preserved mirror with an ivory handle. Notice the exquisite craftsmanship of the carvings. Something this expensive likely belonged to either the captain or a well-to-do passenger. Now, if you'll follow me to the next table..."

Maya tuned out the rest of the museum curator's lecture and wondered how much longer the visit would go on. Deciding to risk a glance at her cell phone, she stepped behind two taller students so she'd be out of sight.

Still another hour to go. I had no idea it would be so totally boring.

Next to her, Lucy sighed loudly and then feigned innocence when Mrs. Brackenberry turned and looked around.

After waiting for their teacher to return her attention to the rusty anchor Dr. Griffith was showing them, Lucy whispered to Maya, "Makes you wish they'd just left the whole freakin' ship at the bottom of the ocean."

Maya smiled. "What's worse, sitting in history class or spending the afternoon here?"

"That's like asking if you'd rather have your period or a stomach virus. They both suck."

Dr. Griffith raised his hand and waved to the group. "Now, if you'll follow me, we'll move on to the next case which contains a fascinating assortment of personal items from the Black Lady, including a pen and a man's pocket watch."

As the class shuffled forward, Maya caught a glimpse of movement in the shadows between two tall display cases. A boy about their own age, maybe a little older, stood there. Since she didn't recognize him from school, she figured he must work at the museum although he seemed to be paying attention to one particular table rather than to Griffith. As she drew closer, she saw his clothes were as out of place as he was: black boots, a worn, white button-down shirt tucked into black denim pants, and black suspenders. His blondish-brown hair fell across his forehead, almost reaching down to his eyes. Although not as big as Stuart or some of the other varsity football players at school, he had a husky build and looked like he could take care of himself in a fight.

Something about him piqued Maya's interest, and she sidled away from Lucy, working her way to the back of the group and off to the side, until she stood only a few feet from him. She glanced his way and smiled, but after a quick look in her direction, the boy returned his gaze to the table he'd been staring at.

Although she didn't consider herself a beauty by any means, the boy's total lack of interest in her surprised Maya and made her even more curious about him. Not to mention a little annoyed.

"Hi. My name's Maya. Do you work here?" She kept her voice low, so as not to attract Mrs. Brackenberry's attention.

The boy jumped slightly and turned to her with wide eyes. "You can see me?"

"Um, hello, you're standing in plain sight. I'm guessing you don't work here, then?"

"Er, no." As if remembering she'd introduced herself, he cleared his throat. "I'm Blake. Blake Hennessy."

"That's a cool name." Maya held out her hand, and after a slight hesitation, Blake shook it. His skin felt cold, and Maya wondered how long he'd been standing in the heavily air-conditioned room.

"So, if you don't work for the museum, what are you doing here?"

"I, um, I can't leave. I've got nowhere else to go."

Maya nodded. It made perfect sense. One of his parents probably worked in the museum, and he had to come here after school. *That must suck, spending afternoons here. I thought I had it bad. At least at the diner I get to eat and drink, and I don't have to stare at boring old junk.*

"I know how that feels. Are you new in town?"

He looked down at the floor and then up again. "I've only been here a few months, but it feels like forever."

Stifling a giggle, Maya nodded. "Yeah, Coronado Bay's like that. Look up 'boring' in the dictionary and you'll find our town. Where are you from?"

Another pause during which his eyes flicked back and forth like a trapped animal's.

Talk about shy. I've never seen a guy so afraid to talk about himself. Then, another thought came to her. *Maybe he's afraid he'll get in trouble talking to me.*

Just when she thought he might not even answer, he said, "Manhattan Island. At least, originally. But this is my home now."

"Lucky you. I was born and raised here. I've only been to New York once, and that was just for a weekend. My family owns the Bay Diner down on Main Street. It's open seven days a week, so we don't get to travel much. I've been to Boston and Cape Cod, too, but only for long weekends. We were supposed to go to Florida once, but--"

"Miss Blair! Please stay with the rest of the class."

Maya looked up and saw Mrs. Brackenberry glaring at her. The class had already moved on to the next exhibit. Behind their teacher, several students, including Lucy, were holding back laughter at Maya's predicament.

"Crap. Gotta go. Nice to meet you, Blake. Maybe we can...?"

Maya's voice trailed off as she realized Blake was no longer standing next to her.

Guess he really was afraid to get in trouble. I wonder where he went?

She hurried to catch up to the class, but her thoughts kept turning back to the mysterious Blake. For the rest of the afternoon she spent more time watching the shadows than paying attention to Dr. Griffith's lectures, to the point where Lucy had to nudge her several times and tell her to stop daydreaming.

No matter what displays she looked at, it was Blake's shy, earnest face she saw. They were almost done with the class trip when she realized something that made her heart jump.

I want to see him again.

* * *

Blake Hennessy watched from behind a heavy cabinet as Maya and the other students shuffled from one exhibit to the next, slowly following a convoluted path to the far side of the long room. A numb feeling still covered his thoughts like sailcloth as he tried to understand how the girl - *Maya, her name is Maya Blair, and her family owns the Bay Diner* - could see him, let alone hear him.

Or touch him.

The memory of her warm flesh on his, the first truly solid thing he'd felt since the Black Lady sank in Coronado Bay, still filled his mind. Even more amazing was the fact that when she was near him, he'd actually grown more solid himself, had been able to feel the cold plaster of the wall, the smooth wood of the cabinets, the tiles beneath his feet. The sensations were so overwhelming he'd barely been able to carry on a sensible conversation.

As the class filed through the exit doors, the loneliness of the past decades came rushing back, a feeling as cold and barren as the bottom of the sea, and one he'd grown too familiar with. He stepped out from behind the cabinet, his incorporeal body expanding to its normal size, and stared at the empty room.

I will see her again. I have to, if only to find out how--

"You look like a fish on a hook. Pray tell, what is so interesting?"

Blake jumped as Gavin Hamlin stepped up beside him.

"Nothing. I--"

Gavin nodded towards the far doors. "Peepin' on the young birds, eh? Saw a couple of nice ones myself. Good enough to eat, right?" He slapped Blake on the back, and then slid his hand down, tightening his grip until Blake flinched. "Now, get your head out from the clouds and get back to work."

Blake pulled free of Gavin's hand, so thankful for not being caught with Maya that he forgot to watch his tongue. "I don't work for you, Gavin. I've got nothing to do with your crazy search."

Fast as a snake striking, Gavin backhanded Blake across the face. Although no sound accompanied the blow, the ceiling lights brightened and then dimmed, and sparks flashed from Gavin's hand.

"You belonged to me the moment you decided to stow away on the Black Lady, runt. And, that won't change until we're all free. The sooner we find the key, the sooner we'll be rid of each other."

Rubbing his cheek, Blake feigned frustration and anger. "Even if we find your damned key, then what? We can't pick it up. We can't unlock the box to get your twice-damned book. We're stuck with the Black Lady forever, and the only difference is we're no longer at the ocean's bottom."

Gavin smiled, a nasty, malevolent twisting of the lips that carried no warmth. "That's where you're wrong, lad. Sooner or later someone will find the key and open the box. If not us, then one of the curators. Curiosity is a powerful thing. And if, by chance, they don't open it, we'll use our powers to do it ourselves. I will have that book. And once I do, I'll restore our bodies and then..."

"And, then what?"

A look of pure madness flashed in Gavin's black eyes. "Never you mind. Suffice to say the world will be a changed place. Now start looking."

Gavin strode away, his black coattails billowing out behind him. Five men, the only other members of the Black Lady's crew to remain on after death, materialized from the shadows and joined their leader in wandering through the exhibition hall, peering under and behind the items salvaged from the ship. Blake didn't know why they bothered, except that Gavin would beat them senseless if they refused. They'd searched the room dozens of times, and Gavin had to know the key, if it wasn't still at the bottom of the ocean, must be inside something, something they couldn't move in their incorporeal state.

Incorporeal...

The moment he thought of it, his memory of Maya, and what she'd done to him, returned. She'd made him solid again. Would her power work on any ghost? If it did, and Gavin found out, he would find a way to keep her near so he'd be able to touch things. To move things.

To find the key and open the box, and the terrible book concealed inside it.

I've got to keep those two as far apart as possible.

Now that he had positive confirmation as to what Gavin had stored inside the box, he had to do whatever he could to make sure Gavin didn't open it.

He couldn't let Gavin get the book.

The world depended on it.

Chapter 4

Every Friday and Saturday night, Coronado Lanes rocked to the sounds of the latest dance tunes as teens of all ages bowled, mingled at the snack bar, or shot pool. The Lanes, as the locals called it, was the only place on the island where kids could hang out after 9 p.m. without getting in trouble for loitering. Psychedelic lights flashed like alien lightning, and the crash of pins mixed with the music to create a solid wall of sound that made it impossible to converse without shouting. Yet, despite the sensory onslaught, the hundred or so teenagers managed to gossip, talk on their cell phones, and send out text messages - often all at the same time.

At the far end from the entrance on Lane Number One, Maya, Lucy, Fiona O'Malley, and Fiona's longtime boyfriend Curtis Devoy sipped sodas and watched as Lucy's current crush, Gary Wallace, reared back and flung his ball down the alley.

* * *

"All I caught was a glimpse of him," Lucy said, referring to Blake Hennessy. "He looked cute, in a Leo DeCaprio kind of way. What was he like?"

"He seemed nice enough," Maya said. "Shy. Kinda lonely, I think. He's new in town."

"So, how come we haven't seen him at school? Or here?" Fiona O'Malley asked. "Or anywhere, for that matter."

Maya shrugged. "Beats me. Maybe he hasn't enrolled yet. Maybe he already graduated. He looked a little older than we are."

"Or maybe," Lucy said, leaning forward in conspiratorial fashion, "he's a millionaire's son, and goes to a private school. Better grab him quick, Maya. He could be your ticket out of this one-fish town."

"Oh, yeah, I'll throw my body at him, and he'll be so taken with me that he'll lead me to his Ferrari and whisk me away to a life of luxury."

"Give him a little pleasure ride of his own, and he just might do that."

Fiona and Lucy laughed and even Maya managed a smile as she shook her head. "With my luck he's a serial killer, and he'll end up driving me to the woods where he'll chop me to pieces."

"Uh, oh." Fiona pointed towards the main doors. "Speaking of bad luck, look who just walked in."

Everyone turned, just in time to see Stuart Newman heading for the snack bar.

"Crap. I can't go anywhere without him showing up. All right, I'm outta here." Maya kicked off her bowling shoes, slid into her sandals, and stood.

"Maya, you can't leave every time Stu's around." Lucy indicated their little group. "He's not gonna do anything with all of us here."

"I know. I'm just not in the mood to deal with him. It's gonna be the same old thing. He'll come over, act nice at first, then get all pissed when I refuse to get back together with him. I just need a few days to clear my head and, hopefully, for him to get over me." Maya tossed ten dollars on the table. "Here, that should cover my shoes and my game, okay? I'll talk to you tomorrow."

Taking advantage of Stuart's back being turned to them as he ordered food, Maya sprinted for the doors and didn't stop running until she reached the far end of the parking lot.

Then, she paused as she realized she didn't want to go home yet.

It's eleven o'clock on a Friday night. My parents aren't expecting me home for another hour. What am I gonna do?

After a moment's consideration, she decided to walk to the end of Main Street and then wander along the beach. The night was warm, and the gentle shushing of the waves always had a calming effect on her nerves.

* * *

As she passed the museum, a ghostly figure called to her from the shadows wrapping the side of the building.

"Maya. Hello."

"Blake." Maya's heart jumped, and she wasn't sure if it was from being startled or from being happy to see him. "What are you doing out here?"

He moved forward, his body appearing to grow more solid as he emerged from the darkness and stepped into the light of the street lamps lining the sidewalk.

"Actually, I was looking for you."

The rapid beat of her pulse turned into a delightful shiver that ran from Maya's head to her toes. "You were looking for me?"

He nodded. "I went by the diner, but it was closed. I didn't know where else you might be, so I've been walking up and down the streets, hoping I'd see you."

"I was with some friends, and I decided to take a walk by the water. Want to join me?" *Oh my God, did I really just say that? What if he says no? What if--*

"I'd love to." He held out his hand, and after a slight hesitation, she took it. The shock of his chilly flesh on hers made her shiver. If anything, his skin felt colder than it had in the museum, as if he'd been holding an icy drink.

Maybe he had a beer, and that's why he was hiding behind the building.

Remembering the conversation with the girls about Blake's age, Maya decided to ask him. "Blake, how old are you?"

"I'm seventeen. I'll be eighteen...I mean, my birthday's in October. The eleventh."

"So how come you don't go to school? Did you graduate early?"

He kept his gaze on his feet as they walked down the hill towards the waterfront. "No. I...dropped out. My family needed the money, so I took a job."

That explains the clothes, and why he was at the museum. He must be a custodian there or something and was too embarrassed to tell me.

"That sucks." New in town, with a crappy job and probably no money to go anywhere or do any of the things the other kids did. No wonder she'd never seen him around.

"That sucks what?"

Maya snorted laughter, "You're weird, but funny."

They reached the end of Main Street and turned right, following the wooden walkway that angled down to the small beach, which hugged the curve of the town's namesake bay. Out on the water a few lights twinkled, red and blue and white, the only parts of the private and commercial boats visible in the dark. A long pier led out to the docking areas, but they bypassed it and instead took the stairs to the beach itself. At the bottom of the steps, Maya paused and took off her sandals.

"I love the way the sand feels on my feet. Especially at night, when it's cool."

Blake bent down and picked up a handful of the rough sand, let it slowly slide through his fingers. "It's been so long since I've felt sand against my skin."

"Dude, you need to get out more." Maya gave him a friendly punch on the shoulder. "I come down here whenever I want to get away from my family, just be alone and think, you know?"

"Yeah."

"I know it's hard to find the time. When I'm home, there's all sorts of distractions, like the computer, and the phone, and the TV. Actually, if you add in school, work, and spending time with my friends, it's a wonder I get any thinking done at all."

They stopped by the water, just out of reach from the tiny waves that stroked the sand in soft whispers.

"I spend a lot of time thinking," he said. "Too much."

"See? You need to get out more. You should come by the Lanes tomorrow night. We'll all be hanging out. We don't even have to bowl, if you don't want to," she added, remembering he might not have any money.

"The Lanes? What's that?"

Maya pointed back towards Main Street. "The bowling alley down past all the stores. It's like, the only place to go in town, unless you count Rollo's Pizza, and they close at ten."

"Will you be there tomorrow night?"

"Yeah, after I get off work. Nowhere else to go, right? We could meet at, like, nine-thirty?"

Blake smiled, an amazing transformation that turned his normally solemn face into something approaching handsome. Maya's stomach did another of those tiny, pleasurable flips.

"I'll be there," he said.

"Great." Before she could say anything else, her cell phone alarm beeped. "Damn. Time to go. If I'm late again, I'll get grounded. I'll see you tomorrow!" Impulsively, she gave him a quick kiss on the cheek and then hurried away, purposely not giving him the chance to try anything else.

Anything else like what? Kissing you back? That's what you wanted, wasn't it?

Yeah, she argued with herself, *but not tonight. I want tonight to end perfectly; and if he'd been a bad kisser or tried to grab a boob or something, it would have ruined everything. For once in my life I want to be the one having the magical night with a boy.*

When she reached the nearest stairs, she stopped. *Oh my god, I'm such an idiot. I never gave him my phone number or email or anything. What if he wants to call me?* She looked back, but the beach was empty. She'd half-hoped he'd still be standing there, like the guys in chick flicks did, watching her walk away.

Get real, Maya. This isn't a movie. He probably had to get home, too. At least I know I'll see him tomorrow. Assuming he doesn't blow me off.

* * *

She started to turn around, then paused. Something seemed...wrong. She stared at the place where they'd been standing when they said goodnight, and that's when she noticed it. Two pairs of footprints led down to the water's edge.

Only hers led away.

For a moment, she thought she might be losing it. Then the answer came to her.

He must have walked back at the water line, and the waves are covering his footprints. That has to be it. Not like he dove into the water or teleported.

Her thoughts returned to Blake's smile and his look of happy surprise when she kissed him.

Another tingle ran through her. *Gotta get home. For once I have a lot to write in my blog, and it's all good!*

Chapter 5

Saturday morning started off badly for Maya, and then grew steadily worse. Her mother woke her up at nine, at least two hours earlier than she'd normally get up, with the news that the upstairs shower had a leak, and she'd have to use the downstairs bathroom.

"You could have left me a note, Mom." Maya buried her head in her pillows in an attempt to block out the bright September sunshine.

"You never see any of my notes," Emily Blair said. "I also need you to run to the store today and pick up a few things. I left the list on the kitchen table. I'd do it, but I have to be at the diner early, thanks to Tessa calling in sick again."

Maya groaned, "I don't have to come in early too, do I?"

Emily laughed. "No, you can go back to sleep. We'll see you at five for the dinner shift."

Except Maya couldn't get back to sleep after her mother left. It seemed as if every resident of Coronado Bay had decided to take advantage of the unseasonably warm, dry weather and torture her. The strident roars and whines of lawn mowers, hedge trimmers, and even boat horns kept intruding, no matter how tightly Maya held her pillows over her ears. After a half-hour of futility, she gave up and accepted her fate.

I'll just get everything done early and then take a nap later, she decided. *Otherwise, I'll be dead on my feet tonight.*

After slipping into a pair of comfortable shorts and a Boston Red Sox T-shirt, tying her sleep-mussed hair into a quick ponytail, and dabbing on just enough lipstick and makeup so she could go out in public without looking like the walking dead, Maya scarfed a breakfast bar and a glass of juice and headed into town.

As she walked past the museum, she saw a sign on the front door. "Closed Sat/Sun for repairs. Reopening Monday."

"That's weird. I wonder what happened."

"Some of the shelving in the new exhibit fell down and caused a big mess."

Maya's heart jumped into her throat, and she inadvertently performed a clumsy pirouette, turning around and stepping backwards at the same time. Her foot slipped off the curb, and before she realized what was happening, she fell into the road. A car horn blared and she instinctively raised her arms as she saw the oncoming vehicle approaching too fast for her to get out of the way.

As the car bore down on her, a strong hand grabbed her arm and pulled her back to the sidewalk. The car sped past, a blur of metal and chrome.

"Are you okay?"

Hazel eyes stared at her. She took a deep breath as she recognized the owner of those eyes. It took two more breaths before she found her voice.

"Blake. Oh my God, you saved my life."

He let go of her arm. "I almost killed you, too. I didn't mean to startle you like that."

"It's not your fault I've got two left feet." Maya rubbed her arm. There'd be bruises there by the afternoon, but at the same time she was sorry he'd let go. "So, what are you up to this morning besides being a hero?"

"I saw you walking up the street and thought I'd come out and say hello. I, um, didn't have a chance last night to say I enjoyed walking with you."

The memory of the previous night's kiss came rushing back, and Maya felt her face grow warm. "I, um, I did, too." *Dumb! Of course you did! You kissed him!*

"Good." He looked down at his feet, then across the street, and anywhere except her face. "Well, I, uh, guess I'll get let you be on your way."

He's going shy on me again. Maya reached out, touched his hand. "I have some errands to run for my mom. If you want, you can tag along. That is, if you've got nothing to do," she added, thinking he might have to help clean up in the museum.

His smile made it seem as if he'd just won the lottery. "Sure. I've got all the time in the world."

"Great." She slid her hand into his. His fingers curled around hers, his cool flesh the perfect counterpart to the hot sun. "Let's go shopping."

* * *

An hour later, they stepped out of the Coronado Pharmacy. Maya had everything on her list, but the prospect of returning home and crawling back into bed no longer seemed so important. For the first time in she couldn't remember how long, she was with a guy she liked, who seemed to like her, and having a good time. She didn't want it to end.

"Hey, do you want to grab a soda or a slice of pizza?" Knowing Blake's financial situation, she knew she'd have to pay, but that didn't matter.

He frowned. "I don't know. Do you need them?"

She slapped his arm. "You really do have a weird sense of humor. Yes, I feel the need for pizza. At least, my stomach does. C'mon, my treat."

Blake came to a stop. "You want to get something to eat?"

"Hello? That's what I've been saying."

A strange look came over Blake's face. He started to say something, then stopped, and then started again. "Before we spend any more time together, I have to tell you something important."

Maya felt like groaning, but kept a neutral look on her face. *Oh, great. He's gonna tell me he has a girlfriend. Or he's gay. I knew this was too good to be true.*

"Sure. Let's sit down over there." She pointed to a nearby bench beneath a wide, shady oak tree. Once they were seated, he took her hands in his, but couldn't meet her eyes as he spoke.

"Maya, the truth is, I am not the person you think I am. I'm...I was born in 1891."

A giggle took shape in Maya's chest but never made it out, as random puzzle pieces came together in her head.

"You're not joking, are you?"

He shook his head. "I wanted to tell you sooner, but, well, at first I thought you knew, since you could see me when no one else could, and then, when I realized you didn't know, I...I didn't know how to say it."

"Oh, my God." Maya's stomach felt like it might fall right to the sidewalk. She stood up and took a step away from the bench, her body reacting while her brain was still trying to process the idea that Blake was...

"You're a ghost?" The words came out on their own. Just speaking them sent a shiver through her body.

He nodded, his face as sad as she'd ever seen it. "I'm sorry I didn't tell you sooner. I should have. It's just..." he let the words trail off, unable to finish his sentence.

"A ghost. You're a ghost." She didn't know whether to run away or to sit down again.

Blake stared at her, and she wondered how she could have not noticed he wasn't a real person.

"It all makes sense now. The appearing and vanishing. The way your footprints disappeared on the beach after I walked away. Unreal. I can't believe my bad luck."

Blake chewed his lip and looked at the ground, reminding her of a frightened puppy who's afraid of being punished. She immediately wished she'd kept her thoughts to herself. He obviously felt bad already, and she'd gone and made it worse.

Okay, so he's a ghost. You already know one ghost, and how many times have you wondered why you hadn't seen others? Well, now you have. So stop acting like a jerk.

The whole idea of his being part of the spirit world still had her a bit freaked, but she felt like she might be able to handle it.

Maya placed a hand on his arm, aware now of why he felt so cold. Once she thought about it, she couldn't believe she hadn't figured it out on her own.

Way to go, Captain Oblivious.

"Blake, it's okay. I didn't mean it was bad luck to meet you. It's just that...you're so nice, it sucks that you're not alive. I wanted to introduce you to my friends. But they won't able to see you."

He looked up, the puppy-dog expression lessened but not gone. "But somehow *you* can see me."

"Yeah. I've been able to see ghosts since I was a little girl. I can hear them and feel them, too."

"That's not all you can do," Blake said. "Even when I'm standing near you, my form becomes solid. The closer we are, the more real I become. When I met you in the museum, it was the first time in over a hundred years I was able to touch, to feel."

"Yeah, I guess that's part of my ability, or whatever you want to call it."

"So you have communicated with other spirits?"

Maya gave a wry smile. "Until now, only one. My grandmother. She died when I was little and started visiting me not long after that. It scared me at first, but I got used to it real quick."

Another thought came to her. "Grandma Elsa told me ghosts usually manifest close to where they died. But I've never seen you around, not until that day at the museum. Where did you come from?"

"I died on the Black Lady when she went down in Coronado Bay. We were on our way to Boston."

"But that was over a hundred years ago. You mean...you were down in the ocean all that time, until they salvaged the ship?" Maya shuddered. She had a touch of claustrophobia, and the thought of being trapped in darkness for an eternity...

"Yes. But time passes differently when you...when you're dead. It's only been since they brought the ship up and took the pieces to the museum that I've begun to notice the days and nights again."

"That's so awful. I can't even stand being stuck in an elevator for very long. I'd have probably gone crazy decades ago."

A strange look passed across Blake's face, something darker than his usual brooding stare. "Some did, I'm afraid."

She wanted to ask him what he meant by that, but just then her stomach gave a loud growl.

"You're very hungry."

"Yeah. C'mon, I still want that pizza. Let's go. We can talk and eat at the same time."

As they headed down the sidewalk, Blake suddenly pointed ahead.

"What's going on over there?"

Diagonally across Main Street from the Pharmacy, where Rollo's Pizza shared a parking lot with a bank, the Grocery Mart, a video store, and Coronado Bay's only Chinese take-out, a group of teenagers stood in front of the Grocery Mart, holding signs and passing out pamphlets to shoppers.

"Those are kids from my school," Maya said, recognizing both the signs and most of the faces. "They're part of Virgin-a-Teens."

"What's that?" he asked, as they crossed over to the parking lot.

"It's a nationwide group of teenagers who are, well, they promote..." Maya paused, feeling an uncomfortable heat rising up her neck and into her cheeks. How was she supposed to bring up sex with a boy she hardly knew, but who triggered the same urges in her the Virgin-a-Teens advocated against.

"Is something wrong?"

"No." *Get your act together, girl! You're not asking him to jump your bones.* That image didn't help, and Maya rushed through the rest of her explanation as fast as she could.

"They try to convince teenagers to wait until marriage before having sex."

"Oh. Isn't that what a good girl should do anyhow? Why do they need to be told?"

Maya stopped walking. "A good girl? Wow, you really are from a different century, aren't you?"

He tilted his head and frowned. "Are things really so dissimilar now? Do most girls give up their virginity easily in this time? Are you still a virgin?"

"That's none of your business!" Seeing the hurt look on Blake's face, Maya softened her tone. "Look, it's not polite to ask someone, especially a girl, a question like that. I--"

"Hey, Blair! You gonna go hand out flyers with the other prudes?"

"Yeah, where's your sign?"

Maya gave a soft groan. Walking towards them were Mary Ellen Gordon and another cheerleader, Kelli Pasternak. Maya hadn't noticed them approaching, or she'd have guided Blake down another row. Now it was too late to avoid a confrontation.

"Who's the new guy, Maya? Does Stuart know about him?"

Before Maya could respond, the two cheerleaders slid into Mary Ellen's sporty new convertible and pulled out of the parking spot with a squeal of tires that made Blake jump. As they drove past, Mary Ellen flipped up her middle finger and shouted, "Smell ya later, loser!"

Staring after the receding car, Blake said, "I would guess those girls are not friends of yours."

"No, they're not." Maya shook her head. "And you can probably guess from their big mouths that the answer to your other question is yes,

I'm a virgin. But I'm not all hung up about it or anything. I mean, if the right guy came along, someone I loved, I wouldn't wait for marriage, you know?"

Blake took her hand and smiled. "Don't let it upset you, Maya. I think it's a good thing."

"You do?"

"Yes. A girl's virtue is her most important asset."

Maya let out a burst of surprised laughter. "Wow, that's a classic. You'll have to tell my friend Lucy that one. She'll argue all night with you that a woman deserves to have the same fun as a man."

"In my time, we had a name for girls like that. We called them whores."

"Whoa! Don't say that to Lucy or you might find a size six shoe in your butt."

"I'll try to remember that. Tell me, are those the pizzas you spoke of?" He pointed at the window of Rollo's Pizza, where several varieties of pizza and calzones sat in the display case.

"Sure are. Best pizza in town. The only pizza in town, too. C'mon, you'll love it."

"Wait." He placed a hand on her arm. "It's food."

"Of course it is. What did you think it was?"

His eyes took on a sad cast. "Maya, I can't eat, remember? I'm a spirit."

"Yeah, but when you're with me, you're solid. So you should be able to eat."

He shook his head. "It doesn't work that way. I'm solid now, but as soon as you move away from me, my body...transforms back to its natural state. And anything inside me..."

It took her a moment to catch on. "Oh. It'll like, fall out, right?"

"Yes. When I'm with you, I can feel and smell, perhaps even taste, but I cannot eat or drink."

For several seconds, neither of them spoke. The early afternoon sun beat down, the last vestige of a summer too stubborn to say goodbye. The sounds of the seagulls overhead, the chanting of the students, the roar of cars passing on Main Street all seemed suddenly too normal to Maya, as if *they* were the things out of place, not the ghost standing next to her.

Determined not to let a small detail ruin their day, she took him by the hand and led him away from the restaurant. "Well, then we don't have to eat pizza. How about if you walk me home instead?"

The depressed look fell away from his face, replaced by a broad smile. "It would be my pleasure." He offered her his arm.

"Well, aren't you the gentleman?" Sliding her arm through his, she led the way back across the parking lot to Main Street.

* * *

Across the street, two long-dead specters watched in truculent surprise as Maya and Blake walked together. To anyone passing by the two beings, they appeared as nothing more than wavering, vertical distortions easily mistaken for heat waves rising from the sidewalk. If the passerby happened to step through the twisting waves, they might have shivered in response to a sudden, momentary chill.

To each other, the ghosts appeared as solid and normal as the world around them.

They kept sharp sailors' eyes on Blake and Maya until the two teenagers disappeared around a corner.

"P'raps this be something Mister Hamlin ought to be knowin' about," said the taller of the two, a gruff-looking, whiskered man who looked to be about sixty, the same as when he'd died.

"Aye." His companion, a wide-shouldered mate with tattooed arms and a scarred neck, nodded. A pipe stuck out from the corner of his mouth, wisps of gray smoke trailing upwards from the bowl. The two figures turned and headed for the museum.

In their wake, a man exiting the barbershop paused as he caught a whiff of cherry-scented tobacco, similar to the kind his grandfather used to smoke. He looked around, but no one else occupied the sidewalk.

Chapter 6

"This is your house?"

Maya and Blake stood in her driveway, Blake looking in awe at the four-bedroom brick and wood colonial.

"Yeah, that's the old homestead. We've lived here since I was like two."

"Your family must be very well off."

Having grown up on an island where they were one of the few families who didn't own second homes in Florida or New York, and who didn't drive a BMW or Mercedes - or both - Maya was taken aback by the thought of someone considering her rich. She wondered what Blake's family had been like. It was hard to tell from talking to him. He dressed in work-style clothes, but then on a boat that made sense. He didn't speak like a sailor, though. His words were well thought out, and his vocabulary better than a lot of the kids she knew, even if it was out of date.

"Actually, we're basic middle class. Even though my parents own the diner, they both have to work just about every day because they can't afford to hire a full-time manager. Compared to a lot of the people in town, we're sort of the opposite of well off."

Blake pursed his lips. "Truly things have changed."

Before she could respond, Maya's cell phone rang. Blake jumped and stared as she pulled out the phone and glanced at the screen. "It's my mom. Shhh. I'm not supposed to have boys over when no one's home."

Clicking the talk button, she said in a louder voice, "Hi, Mom. What's up? Huh? Yeah, I got everything you wanted. Yes, I'll be there on time. I'm getting ready right now. Bye!"

After making sure she'd closed the connection, Maya turned to Blake. "Sorry, but I gotta get to work. We're still on for tonight, right?"

Still gazing at the cell phone, he said, "Yes. Coronado Lanes."

"Nine-thirty. See you then." Maya stepped back, but stopped when Blake moved forward and grasped her hands. Before she knew what was happening, he leaned in and kissed her, a long, full kiss that left her speechless when he finally broke it off.

"Nine-thirty. Goodbye, Maya." He turned and walked away, his body gradually fading into nothingness as he left her sphere of influence, until nothing of him remained except an exciting tingle on her lips and tongue.

Shaking herself out of her daze, Maya went inside and quickly got dressed for work. As she did so, her mind kept replaying Blake's kiss, followed by a question she couldn't answer.

How stupid is it to fall for a ghost?

* * *

Silence ruled the hallways of the Maritime Museum once it closed for the night. Lit only by emergency lights, the high-ceilinged hallways and exhibition rooms acted as a passive alarm system, reflecting and amplifying the slightest of sounds from one room to the next, in the same manner as a system of caves. For that reason, Gavin Hamlin always held back from searching for the lost key until he was sure all the employees had taken their leave for the night. He never wasted his time, though. Instead, he spent countless hours contemplating the Black Lady exhibit, wracking his brain to come up with another idea as to where the key might be hidden, and how to get it.

He refused to entertain the possibility it still lay on the bottom of the ocean. No, it would be close to the book, he was sure of that. The magiks imparted into the key and book ensured they'd remain close to each other.

As for the book, it sat inside its locked box right on the center table, drawing his eyes and relentlessly mocking his impotence.

"Sir, we hates to bother you, but there's somethin' we think you ought to hear."

As he turned towards the two sailors approaching him in the semi-darkness of the room, Gavin did his best to hide his annoyance at being disturbed. No sense taking his frustrations out on them. He'd need their full cooperation when he finally opened the thrice-damned box.

"What is it?"

"We happened upon young Mister Hennessy leaving the building today," said Anton Childs, the oldest of all the sailors and the closest thing Gavin had to a confidant, as well as second in command. "Thought it a might odd for any of us to go about in the daylight, let alone venture away from that which ties us here, so we took it upon ourselves to follow him."

Gavin frowned as he considered their words. *What could Hennessy be up to?* He'd never trusted the boy. His story of stowing aboard the Black Lady because he'd run away from home didn't seem in keeping with his general demeanor. Oh, he'd worked hard enough in the couple of days before they'd sunk, but there'd been something about him...something that set Gavin's nerves a-twitter whenever the boy was near.

Boy. Strange to think of him that way, with Blake but two years younger. Two years, but a world of difference between us.

"What did he do?"

"Believe it or not, he met up with a girl. Human, she was, and damn nice on the eyes, to boot." Childs made an hourglass figure in the air with his hands.

"Ayuh," agreed Victor Fogg, speaking around his pipe. "I'd show her a thing or two if I were alive."

"A human? That's impossible." Gavin lifted his hands and blue sparks of energy crackled from his fingertips. "What kind of fool do you play me for?"

The two sailors, both twice Gavin's age, but as afraid of him in death as they'd been in life, backed away. "No, sir, 'tis no joke." Childs shook his head. "Human, she was. We saw other humans speak to her, and to Hennessy, as well."

Through his anger, Gavin felt a new emotion surge forward, something he hadn't felt since he and others first manifested in the museum.

Hope.

If Hennessy's somehow found a way to interact with the real world...

Gavin smiled, taking silent pleasure in the fearful way the two men reacted to his expression.

"I think we need to talk to Mister Hennessy."

Chapter 7

Maya started counting the minutes to the end of her shift when she still had two hours to go. The dinner crowd hadn't been bad - she'd seen worse for a Saturday night - but it was bad enough to stop her from asking if she could leave a little early. That meant staying until eight-thirty, which meant she'd only have an hour to race home, shower, get dressed, and race back across town to the bowling alley.

She couldn't even ask to use the car because she still wasn't old enough to drive after nine. Not that her parents would let her take it. Her father insisted on driving to the bank to make each night's deposit, even though crime was nearly non-existent in Coronado Bay.

God, she couldn't wait until she had enough money to buy her own car, even if it ended up being a rust bucket with four bald tires.

Anything was better than asking for rides or walking.

Forty-three minutes. She grabbed a bowl of clam chowder and delivered it to table twelve. With nearly all the tables and booths filled, the noise level in the diner made it all but impossible to hear anything except the sounds she'd trained herself to distinguish from the racket: the *ding* of the kitchen bell, the words "Waitress!" or "Miss!" shouted by a customer.

"Maya!"

Or her name being called.

She glanced at her mother, saw her waving frantically.

A small hole opened in her stomach, threatening to swallow her from the inside out. The look on her mother's face indicated the news wouldn't be good. Which could only mean one thing.

Please. Not tonight. Please. If there's a God in heaven...

"Was that who I think it was?" Maya asked, as her mother hung up the phone behind the register.

"I'm sorry, Maya. Annabelle..."

"Isn't coming in, right? What, she's sick, too?"

Emily Blair shook her head. "No, she had a car accident. She's all right, but the doctor said she has to stay home tonight, just to be sure."

It's not fair! Maya wanted to shout it out loud, but she knew how it would sound. Petulant. Selfish. *Typical teen-age reaction.* So she clamped her mouth shut. But her face must have given her away because her mother immediately said something.

"I know that look. Did you have plans tonight?"

'Plans' was her mother's way of asking if she had a date. "Kind of, yeah. We're supposed to meet at the Lanes."

"Well, just call him and say you'll be a couple of hours late. Problem solved." Before Maya could respond, her mother zipped out from behind the counter to seat an elderly couple who'd just come in.

Maya closed her eyes and took a deep breath. *If only it were that easy. Too bad there's no cellular service for the dead.*

Ding! "Order up! Maya, let's go. Get a move on!"

Fists clenched, Maya opened her eyes and got back to work.

* * *

Gavin Hamlin stepped out of the shadows, a nasty, mean expression on his face, just as Blake entered the museum's main foyer.

"Where you going, lad?" As he spoke, four of his men entered the room and made a rough circle around Blake.

Caught off guard by their appearance, Blake stammered a reply. "I, um, was just heading outside to walk the beach. It...it helps me think."

"Sounds like a bucket of manure to me. I heard tell you were out and about with a human today. Might be that you're heading off to see her again?"

Someone saw us! Blake's mind raced. There was no sense in lying, but at the same time, he had to protect Maya's identity if he could. Best to put on a show of force and maybe take Hamlin's mind off Maya. If it meant some physical punishment, so be it. Better him than her.

"You don't own me, Hamlin. I can go where I want."

Gavin moved closer, his hands balled into fists. Sparks arced from his clenched fingers, creating miniature fireworks in the dim light. "That's where you're wrong, lad. I do own you, until such a time as you can show me otherwise. Now, I'm going to ask you a question, and you'd better have an answer. How were you and the girl able to talk to each other?"

Something rose up inside Blake, the old anger he'd inherited from his mother, along with her hatred for the entire Hamlin clan and what they'd stood for.

"Piss off."

Without warning, Hamlin's left fist flashed forward, striking Blake square in the stomach. Flashes of lightning exploded where incorporeal substances met, and Blake doubled over with a cry of pain. Hamlin swiftly followed with another punch, a right hand to Blake's jaw that knocked him sideways while more bursts of light lit up the room.

Blake looked up at Hamlin. "I'm not telling you a damn thing." Each word sent arrows of pain through his cheek and guts, but he refused to let it show.

The tall, dark-haired young man laughed - an evil sound that made Blake cringe. "That's too bad for you, but good for me. I can do this all night, or until you talk, whichever comes first. Hold him down, boys."

* * *

For the next fifteen minutes, anyone walking past the Maritime Museum would have thought something was wrong with the lights, or perhaps someone was working with welding equipment.

None of them would have suspected a ghost was taking a terrible beating.

* * *

Maya sipped a soda and wondered what to do. She'd hoped Blake would be waiting for her at the bowling alley, even though she'd been two hours late. But there was no sign of him anywhere. And it wasn't like she could ask any of her friends if they'd seen him.

He could have done the Hamster Dance in front of them, and they'd have never known.

"You gonna bowl or just stand there?" Lucy asked.

Maybe he went down to the beach. He seems to like walking there. "No, I think I'm gonna go home. Work sucked, and I'm tired. I'll catch you tomorrow, okay?"

Lucy frowned. "Are you sure you're all right? I could--"

"Hey, Lucy! C'mon, you're up!"

Lucy raised her middle finger towards Gary, one of the many unladylike habits she somehow managed to pull off without seeming crass. "I'll be right there. Don't get your panties in a bunch."

"Go ahead, Luce. I'm fine." Maya forced a smile.

Lucy gave her a close look, but in the end the lure of fun and flirting won out. "All right. We'll talk tomorrow." She gave Maya a quick kiss and then ran back to the lane and grabbed a ball from the rack.

Maya watched them for a moment longer, tempted to stay and enjoy herself. After all, she deserved a night of fun. But even stronger was the feeling of guilt at having stood Blake up. She owed it to him to try and find him and apologize.

God, could this night get any worse?

With a sigh, she headed for the exit.

* * *

Blake watched as Gavin and his men passed through the museum doors and out into the night. Guilt weighed on him as heavily as the Atlantic waters on a drowning man. He'd tried to hold out, but in the end Gavin's punishment was too severe. He'd begged for mercy, told them everything he knew. How Maya had the ability to see and speak with ghosts. How being near her enabled a ghost to be solid again. Gavin hadn't believed him and had beaten him a second time for lying.

Afterwards, however, one of the other sailors, the old timer named Childs, had pulled Gavin aside and spoken with him. They'd kept their voices low, but thanks to the way sounds carried in the cavernous room, Blake managed to hear most of what they said.

"'Tis possible, it is, sir. I've heard tell of such things. My pa, he was from the old country. Said 'twas something some folk could do. Most times it got them burned at the stake for witchcraft, it did."

"If what you're saying is true, then simply by keeping her near us we could regain our corporeality and actually search the museum for the key."

"Aye, I guess. But there's more to it than that. 'Ccording to the tales my Pa told me, if the lass in question be a virgin, then taking her womanly blood would make you whole again, forever."

A note of black desire had crept into Gavin's voice. Blake felt unclean just from hearing it. "You mean, if I make this girl's virginity my own, I'll be...human again?"

"That's what the stories say. I've never met a witch, so I can't say with any authority as to the truth o' that. But then, so far the tale seems true enough, eh?"

Gavin eyes had flicked towards Blake. "I wonder if he knows this girl well enough to say if she's a virgin?"

"I don't know about her, but her friends are." Anton Childs stepped forward. "When we was watching them, we saw them talking with a whole boodle of lasses. And they was holding signs in the air. I couldn't read them all, but I saw the word virgin on some of them."

"Really?" Gavin's voice indicated he didn't believe the sailor's story.

"Swear on me mother's grave, sir. T'aint no hornswaggle. 'Twas the opposite of the docks when we was alive. There the whores announced themselves. P'raps here the virgins do."

Chuckling softly, Gavin had rubbed his hands together. "I think maybe I need to meet this girl. Take me to this bowling alley."

After the other ghosts left, Blake attempted to get up, but his arms and legs refused to cooperate. *I've got to warn Maya!* Marshalling all his will, he commanded his body to sit up.

Nothing happened.

It's as if Gavin's punches drained my energy.

The idea didn't seem all that outlandish to Blake. After all, Gavin was a sorcerer, descended from a long line of even more powerful sorcerers. That was the reason Blake had followed him to New York in the first place, to keep his promise to his mother and stop

Gavin from bringing the book to Boston. Technically, he'd failed at that, but he'd taken solace in knowing the danger had ended with the sinking of the Black Lady.

Until those damned scientists dragged us from our graves!

Now it looked like he might fail again. If he couldn't keep Gavin and Maya apart, then all he'd managed to do was delay the inevitable by a couple of centuries.

I can't let him win.

Gritting non-existent teeth, he moved his arms under his chest, and pushed with all his strength.

Chapter 8

Maya brushed cool sand off her feet and slipped her sandals back on. She'd walked the entire beach, hoping Blake would appear. Naturally, she'd seen no sign of him.

Talk about bad luck with guys. It's not enough that I can't make a connection with any boys in my school. Now I manage to screw things up with a ghost who hasn't seen a girl in one hundred years. Maybe I should start dating girls, like Alison Keel from history class.

She knew that wouldn't happen, though. The two times she'd experimented with Lucy behind the Lanes had convinced her she was totally straight, unlike some of her friends. Not that it grossed her out or anything, but the turn-on factor just hadn't been there, even after a few wine coolers.

So, girls are out. Apparently guys are out. And now even ghosts are out. That doesn't leave much. Maybe I should just start collecting cats, like old lady McCann down the street.

She started toward her house, then changed her mind and headed back up Main Street. *One more trip past the museum, in case--*

A hand came down hard on her shoulder and spun her around. Even as she started to scream, her attacker grabbed her by the shirt and threw her to the ground.

"Shut yer mouth, girl, or I'll shut it for good."

Maya scooted backwards as the heavy-set man approached her. A jagged scar ran across one cheek. Something moved behind him, and she realized he wasn't alone. A second man stood there, dressed just as shabbily as his partner.

She stopped screaming and took a deep breath as the first man bent down, his hands ready to grab her. Focusing on a spot in the middle of his chest, she lashed out with one foot and then scrambled to her feet as the man let out a surprised grunt and stumbled backwards into his companion.

Rubbing his chest, the man glared at her. "Now you're in for it, witch." Hands raised, he lunged forward.

Maya waited until the last second before kicking again. This time she caught him on his left knee, and he cried out in pain, a scream that abruptly turned into a coughing groan when her second kick landed right in his crotch, sending him to his knees.

Turning to the second man, who was smaller and thinner, Maya shouted, "C'mon, asshole! Try me!"

The man took a step forward, and for a moment Maya thought he might really come at her. She crouched down, her lessons in blocking and kicking clear as day in her head thanks to hours of practice. Then he turned and ran around the corner, disappearing in the shadows of a tall hedge.

With the immediate danger gone, her adrenaline subsided and the realization that she'd been attacked - attacked right on Main Street! - hit her like a punch to the stomach.

What if there's more of them?

Without waiting to see if the first attacker was back on his feet, she ran up Main Street to the diner, where her father was just coming out the back door to make the nightly bank deposit.

"Dad!"

The sight of him, and the safety he represented, triggered her tears, which made her rushed explanation even harder to understand.

"Whoa, settle down. Are you hurt? Did they touch you?"

Maya nodded against his chest. "I'm okay. They knocked me down. I kicked one of them in the balls and ran." She wrapped her arms around her father, relishing the strength and security of his presence. Even his odor, part sweat and part food, made her feel safer.

Keeping a firm grip on her, Roger Blair guided his daughter back into the diner, where he sat her down and then called the police.

Ten minutes later, Police Chief Clayton Finley, a gruff, pot-bellied man whose daughter had been Maya's babysitter back in middle school, pulled up outside, lights flashing atop his olive-green SUV.

"I've got Ted Barry cruising the side streets," he said, after making sure Maya hadn't been hurt. "I didn't see anything on my way here, so that fellow whose 'nads you smashed must not have been hurt too badly. Or maybe his friend came back for him. You didn't happen to see a car, did you?"

Maya shook her head. "No. I was just walking, and all of a sudden they hit me from behind."

Finley made notes in a small pad. He had a habit of licking his pencil each time he wrote, which started to annoy Maya after the first couple of times. "Prob'ly hiding in the hedges, waitin' for someone like you to walk by alone. Dammit, Maya, you should know better than to be out by yourself this late at night."

"I was on my way home. I didn't know our town was so dangerous I needed a police escort."

"Easy, Maya," Roger said, patting her hand. "Clayton, we both know the kids always walk around at night. These streets are supposed to be safe."

Finley shrugged beefy shoulders. "Every year the big city gets a little closer to our island. I keep telling the mayor we need more help. I can't do this job with just two officers."

"Well, I'll take Maya home tonight. Does she have to make a formal statement or something?"

The Chief shook his head. "Nah. Not unless we catch the bastards. Then I'll ask her to come in and identify them. Sure you can't remember anything else?" he asked Maya.

"No." She'd already given the Chief a description of the two men.

"All right. I guess I don't have to tell you to stay off the streets at night for a while, unless you've got friends with you. Sounds like these two mighta been homeless or something. Heaven knows why they came here."

God, why wouldn't he shut up? All she wanted to do was go home and crawl into bed with a hot cup of tea. "No, I'll be careful from now on," she said, more to reassure her father than anything else. Truth was, she knew none of her friends, or her, were going to stay off the streets just because some derelicts tried to mug her.

"Then, I'll get going. We'll patrol the area extra tonight, just in case. Maybe we'll get lucky and catch them heading back to wherever they came from. 'Night, Roger."

"'Night, Clayton. Thanks, again." Roger looked down at Maya. "Ready to go?"

"God, yes. Um, do we have to tell Mom?"

"What do you think?"

Maya rubbed her eyes.

"I think it's gonna be a long night."

* * *

"Damn you idiots to the seven Hells!" Gavin shook his fists at Nigel Murphy and Ian Powell as he stalked back and forth across the museum foyer. Miniature explosions of electricity, like tiny balls of St. Elmo's fire, shot from his knuckles, illuminating the sailors' frightened faces. "You let a girl best you in a fight!"

"Bloody girl wasn't supposed to fight back," Powell muttered. Murphy remained silent, the pain of Maya's well-placed kicks still fresh in his mind.

Gavin pointed a glowing finger at Powell, and the sailor cringed. "I don't care if she carried a bag of weapons and stood ten feet tall. She's a damned *girl*. You had her on the ground. For the love of God, all you had to do was fall on her."

"You don't understand, sir. She was like some kind of witch, she was."

Murphy nodded his agreement at his companion's statement.

"A witch? What did she do, cast a spell of idiocy on you both? Get the hell out of here before I show you what real magik is and return you to the watery graves I dragged you from." Gavin turned his back, and the two men who'd once been deckhands on the Black Lady hurried away before he could change his mind.

"What now, Mister Hamlin?" Victor Fogg, who'd been watching from a safe distance while Gavin berated the sailors, asked.

"What now?" The tall youth stared out the wide windows of the museum. A pale, luminescent corona surrounded his body, as if stray moonbeams followed him and spotlighted his every move.

"Now, I take things into my own hands."

* * *

From his hiding place behind a wall of bookshelves, Blake listened to Gavin and clenched his fists until they glowed like a steam engine's coals. Maya was still safe, but it was only a matter of time before Gavin got hold of her.

No, I cannot let it happen. No matter what the cost, I must protect her. This I vow.

Chapter 9

On Sunday morning, Maya almost missed church. She didn't know it at the time, but her running late initiated a chain of events that would eventually lead to several deaths.

Blissfully ignorant and still muddleheaded from a poor night's sleep, she opened her eyes to bright sunshine, the caress of a warm breeze across her skin, and the smell of fresh-mown grass trickling in through her open window.

It should be cold and rainy, because that's how I feel inside.

Sleep had been a long time in coming the previous night, between her guilt over standing up Blake and the residual adrenaline in her body from the violent encounter on Main Street. She'd texted Lucy before going to bed, but didn't expect to hear anything until later in the day. Sundays, Lucy usually slept until just before she had to be at work, and then didn't get a chance to talk on the phone until her break later in the afternoon. Maya's Sundays usually meant being up at nine-thirty to get ready for church. She went early because her parents attended the late afternoon services, during the lull between the lunch and dinner crowds, while Maya covered the cash register.

Still staring at the ceiling, Maya groaned at the sound of the town clock tower chiming ten times. That meant she had about ten minutes to wash up and eat.

For a split second she contemplated staying in bed. There was a good chance her parents wouldn't mind, not after the night she'd had. But if she used being tired or nervous as an excuse to skip church, there was a good chance they wouldn't let her hang with Lucy later.

Time to drag my sorry butt out of bed, then.

Five minutes later, dressed in church-acceptable shorts and blouse, her hair tied back in a pony tail, and extra makeup covering the circles under her eyes, Maya sat down at the table and gulped down a bowl of cereal while she read the note her mother had left her.

If you're not feeling well this morning, stay home and rest. I'll call later and see how you're doing. If you need anything, let me know.

Maya snorted. "No way I'm staying home," she said through a mouthful of Rice Krispies. In fact, she was kind of looking forward to work. Maybe Master Spiegel, her karate instructor, would stop by like he sometimes did on Sundays. She wasn't sure she could wait until class on Monday to tell him how she'd handled her attackers. She'd been taking lessons for two years, but between work, school, and hanging out with her friends, she'd never made the progress she wanted to, or that he expected of her.

I can't wait to see the expression on his face. Maybe I'm not as bad as I thought I was.

Laughing at his imagined reaction, she hurried out the door and down the street towards Our Lady of Sorrows, Coronado Bay's only Methodist church.

Halfway there, a familiar figure stepped out from behind a tree and waved to her.

"Blake!" She picked up her pace, closing the distance between them, grateful to see a friendly smile on his face.

I hope that means he's not mad at me.

"Good morning, Maya," he said, his voice as happy as his face.

"Hi. I'm, like, really sorry about last night. My parents made me work late, and I couldn't call you 'cause you don't have a phone, and then I went to the Lanes looking for you and then walked down to the beach and then these guys attacked me, and--" Maya stopped, belatedly realizing her words were pouring from her mouth in machine-gun fashion.

"It's okay," Blake said. Then his face turned serious. "But I have something important to talk to you about. I--"

At that moment, the church bells pealed, announcing there was only a couple of minutes until services started.

"C'mon, I can't be late or Pastor Harris will tell my parents!" Maya grabbed Blake's hand and ran down the sidewalk to the church, not pausing until they opened the heavy wooden doors and stepped into the incense-scented semidarkness. A few heads turned and cast disapproving glances as the door banged shut behind them.

"We'll sit in the back," Maya whispered, pointing to a half-empty pew. "That way we can leave as soon as the service is over."

"But I--"

"Sshh!" Maya put a finger to her lips and pulled Blake down into the seat next to her. "Tell me later."

For the next fifty minutes, Maya did her best to pay attention to the sermon, but found her eyes continually drawn to the boy sitting next to her. His frigid hand was a constant reminder of his presence, not to mention something of a relief in the warm, stuffy church. Every time their eyes found each other, a little tingle shot through her and made her squirm in her seat.

Even when he faced forward, as he did most of the time, seemingly enthralled by the pastor's sermon, he held her attention. She took time to study his profile. His pug nose, which seemed almost babyish when viewed straight on, had a more mature look from the side. His light brown eyebrows bent forward as he concentrated on the pastor's words. His eyelashes, so ordinary from the front, were in actuality long and delicate.

She wondered what he was thinking. Had he attended church regularly before he died? How did church today differ from his time? Had he always been so serious, or did that come from being a ghost?

Grandma Elsa still jokes with me all the time. Maybe Blake was just a shy kid, or maybe it had something to do with drowning the way he did. That had to be a horrible experience.

Having something other than the Reverend's sermon to concentrate on helped the time go by, and before she knew it services came to an end. As soon as it did, she and Blake made a hurried exit.

Maya didn't want to get stuck talking to anyone, especially since she still had no idea how she'd handle explaining Blake's presence.

"Can we talk now?" Blake asked, as they descended the long stone front steps of the church.

"Sure. I--" The chime of Maya's cell phone interrupted her. "Hang on. Hello?"

"Maya? Where are you?"

"Just leaving church, Mom. What's up?"

"Can you come right over? It seems like half the town decided to go out for breakfast today, and the other half is probably leaving church with you and heading over here."

"Sure. Be right there." Turning to Blake, she said, "I'm so sorry. My parents need me at work right away."

He looked distressed. "But I really need to speak with you. It's important."

"Can it wait until later? I get off work at five. Meet me at my house. We'll have the place to ourselves for hours. You remember how to get there?"

He nodded. "Five o'clock. I'll be there when you get home."

"Cool. See you later." She blew him a kiss and took off at a fast walk towards Main Street. She was all the way to the corner when she remembered that without her nearby, Blake had just turned invisible in front of dozens of people.

Well, I didn't hear anyone scream. That's good, I guess. Gotta be more careful next time. God, dating a ghost is harder than dating a regular guy.

Still preoccupied with the image of Blake fading away in front of the Sunday congregation, Maya didn't notice the tall, dark-haired young man standing in front of the diner until she bumped into him.

"Oh! I'm so sorry. I'm like a total flake today."

The man, who looked about twenty or so, smiled. "That's all right. There are worse things than having a pretty girl step on your toes."

Maya tried to think of a witty come back, but her mind went blank as she stared into the stranger's movie-star dark eyes. He looked like he'd just stepped out of one those hip TV shows where wild teenagers spend their whole lives hanging out at the beach or in the mall. *More like one of those movies about angst-ridden vampires who pine to be human again,* she thought. His fancy white dress shirt, worn untucked, and the waist-length black jacket with the silver buttons added to the look.

"What's your name?"

It took her a moment to understand he was talking to her.

"Oh, um, Maya. Maya Blair."

"Pleased to meet you." He nodded to her. "My name is Gavin Hamlin."

"Hi. Did you come out of the diner?"

"No, I was just walking the streets, getting to know the town."

"Oh, are you new here?"

"Yes. My family...owns a business in Boston, and I'm here for a while working on some contracts."

Maya gave a small laugh. "Don't take this the wrong way, but you look a little young for that. Shouldn't you still be in like, college or something?"

Gavin shrugged. "I attended university for a while, but..." He let the words trail off, and then gave Maya a quick wink. She smiled.

"Wasn't for you, huh? Sometimes I think school's not my--"

"Maya!" Her mother poked her head out the door. "Hurry up. You're already late."

"I'll be right in, Mom. God, gimme a minute." Hoping her embarrassment didn't show too much, she turned back to Gavin. "I, um, gotta go."

"I understand. Perhaps we could meet later?"

"I'd love that." *Don't gush, Maya!* Then she remembered Blake would be at her house after work. "Um, but I'm getting together with friends later. How about we meet tomorrow afternoon? Around four-thirty?"

His lips curled up in a half-smile that promised hard, rough kisses. "I'll be counting the hours."

"Um, cool, I, uh--"

Maya's mother saved her from further embarrassment by opening the door again. "Maya! We've got tables waiting! Shake a leg."

"Sorry. I *really* gotta go. See you tomorrow." She fled into the noisy safety of the diner before her tongue made her sound like a complete spaz. But he'd been so handsome! Then there was no time to even think about the encounter as her mother pushed an apron into her hands and told her to bring coffees to table seven.

It wasn't until her shift ended that she realized she hadn't given Gavin her number, or gotten his.

Great. That's twice this week you've acted like you've never met a guy before. At least Blake, thanks to his being dead and all, had a way of finding her.

The only thing Gavin knows is where you work. Which means hanging out by the diner after karate practice tomorrow, hoping he'll show up.

That thought led to another. *What about Blake?*

She knew what Lucy would say. *"It's a no-brainer. You just started dating Blake. You're not married to him. You're not even going steady or anything. You're totally free to see someone else. Especially a McHottie like Gavin."*

The imagination-Lucy was right. She wasn't tied to Blake. Forget the fact he was a ghost. They hardly knew each other. Besides, what if Gavin turned out to be the right guy for her. How would she know if she didn't at least go on one date with him?

The weird thing was Gavin was the total opposite of Blake. The fresh-faced, serious kid vs. the darkly sensual man. Day vs. night. Good guy vs. stereotypical bad guy. You knew they'd both open a door for you, but you also knew Gavin would check out your butt, maybe even snap a pic of it on his cellphone, as you walked past. Blake would always be there for you. Gavin would burn like fire for a month, and then you'd find out he had a girlfriend back in Boston. Or maybe two. Blake would become friends with your friends. Gavin would try to date them.

And yet somehow, she felt drawn to Gavin, as if a dark, dangerous gravitational field surrounded him and it was pulling her in.

The Lucy in her head laughed and rolled her eyes. *"So do the horizontal mambo with Gavin and then go back to Blake."*

"God, Lucy, all you think about is sex."

"Excuse me?"

Maya turned from hanging up her apron and saw an elderly woman by the bathroom door giving her a confused look.

"Um, I said, this hook is loose; it'll fall off next."

The spinster-type stared for a moment longer then went into the ladies room, shaking her cotton-topped head.

Great. Now I'm talking to myself. Get a grip, Maya. What are you gonna tell Blake when you see him?

By the time she reached her house, she still had no answer to that question.

Chapter 10

When she saw Blake sitting on her front porch, a wave of guilt washed over Maya. How could she think about hurting him? He already looked like a scared puppy, hiding in the corner, afraid someone might kick him.

"Hi, Blake." She put extra sunshine into her greeting, and he rewarded her with a smile.

"Hello, Maya. I got here early. I hope that's all right. I didn't really have anywhere else to go."

"No, that's fine." Maya rummaged through her pockets until she located her house keys. She found it really didn't bother her, either. Yet, if Stuart had done something like that while they were dating, she'd have bitched him out, told him how creepy it was.

Is that because Blake is dead and no one could see him there anyhow? Or because he's a decent guy, and Stuart was kind of a creep?

"Is this a good time to talk? I really need to tell you what's going on. You could be in--"

"So, this is the guy you dumped me for?"

Crap. Not now. Wondering if thinking about Stuart acted like a spell and called him to her, she turned to face her ex-boyfriend, feeling her face already drawing into a frown.

"What, you're spying on me now, Stuart? Why don't you just get a life and stay out of mine?" She walked across the porch and stood at the top step, staring down at him. A cold presence against her back told her Blake was standing close to her.

Stuart Newman's square face turned red as he approached the stairs. "Don't tell me what to do. You've got some nerve after you lied right to my face about seeing someone else."

"I never lied to you." She had to bite down on her lip to keep the rest of her sentence to herself. *At least not about the dating part.*

"I call bull on that." He pointed past her. "And there's the proof, just like Mary Ellen told me."

"Oh, so now you believe the Wicked Slut of the West instead of me? You're getting more whacked by the day. Just go home and leave us alone."

Stuart came up the steps until he was only inches from her. "Oh, I'll leave you alone. Soon as I teach your little friend here that it ain't okay to steal someone's girlfriend."

Before Maya knew what had happened, Stuart pushed her to the side and charged Blake, his right hand already formed into a fist and swinging.

Blake just stood still, a blank expression on his face, as if resigned to his fate.

Maya watched with sick fascination as Stuart's fist passed right through Blake and kept going. Thrown off balance by finding only air where he expected solid matter, Stuart's body followed his hand, falling forward and hitting the railing with his waist. With a surprised grunt, he flipped over the railing, looking very much like the football players he tackled so well for the Coronado Bay Pirates each Saturday.

He landed hard, his head striking one of Emily Blair's garden statues with a sound like someone dropping a melon on the sidewalk.

To Maya, it seemed as if the world stopped. Nothing moved. The only thing she heard was a buzzing in her ears. Even the air paused, like an invisible animal ready to pounce.

Then, her lungs heaved in a deep breath, and the world turned back on.

"Oh, crap." She ran down the steps. Stuart lay atop her mother's azaleas, his head next to a cement mushroom, his eyes closed. She slid her hand under his head. A sizeable lump was already forming, but her hand came back free of blood.

"He's okay, I think. Just stunned. But I better call a doctor."

For someone who had no actual blood, Blake looked paler than normal. "Maya, I'm sorry. I didn't mean for this to happen. Let me help you."

She shook her head. "It's not your fault. He's an asshole. That's why I dumped him. But it'll be better if you're not here when he wakes up. Hopefully he won't remember what happened."

"But--"

"I'm sorry, Blake. I know you want to talk. I wanna talk, too. But I have to go call an ambulance, so you've gotta get out of here. I promise, we'll sit down and talk about whatever you want."

"Tomorrow?"

"No. Tomorrow I've got karate class after school and...and then a study group," she finished, hating the guilt demon squirming inside her, hating herself for lying to him. Why couldn't she just be like Lucy and cheat without a conscience? "But definitely Tuesday. Tuesday for sure. Now go." She pulled out her cell phone and dialed 911.

Stuart moaned and moved his head.

"Hurry. He's waking up."

When Blake didn't answer, Maya glanced up and saw he'd already left.

It never occurred to her he might still be close by.

Blake watched from behind the neighbor's house as the white vehicle with the flashing lights pulled into Maya's property. He'd recognized the word ambulance when she'd said it, but the screaming vehicle that arrived had nothing in common with the ambulances of his time other than the color. Two men in white uniforms examined the boy Maya called Stuart, placed him on a rolling table, and then slid him into the vehicle. Maya and one of the men, who Blake assumed was a doctor of some kind, got in the back with Stuart and shut the doors. The other doctor drove the vehicle away.

Once Maya was gone, Blake stepped out into the open, knowing he couldn't be seen by anyone else.

What do I do now? Sooner or later Gavin or his men will find Maya again. And whatever they do to her, it will be bad. Very bad.

He had to find a way to get her to listen to him. But it seemed fate had something else in mind and was taking personal pleasure in throwing obstacles in his way. And, Maya's personality didn't help. Unlike the demure, sedentary girls of his time, she never sat still for a moment. She also talked more - much more - than the girls he'd known when alive, making it hard to even start the conversation he needed so badly to finish.

None of that matters. I've got to find a way. If anything happens to her, it will be my fault.

Frustration boiled over. He kicked out at a nearby lawn chair, which remained perfectly stable as his foot passed through. "Damn!"

Next to him, sparks burst from an electrical socket on the outside of the house.

Blake's anger drained away as he stared at the smoking outlet. *Did I do that?*

He'd previously thought only Gavin could affect the physical world, that it was somehow related to his use of magic when alive. *What if it's something all ghosts can do? Something I could do again?*

And if he could do it again, could he learn to control it the way Gavin did? More importantly, would it be enough to stop Gavin and his plans?

* * *

Maya lay in bed, her cell phone cradled against one ear, only half-concentrating on her conversation with Lucy. Her body and head were at war, and it was distracting her to no end. All her body wanted to do was go to sleep, but her brain resisted. It was in hyper drive, unable to slow down after everything that had happened.

"So, what did they say at the hospital?"

"What?" Maya tried to focus on Lucy's words. It sounded as if she were eating popcorn, which made the whole listening thing doubly difficult. "Oh. He's fine. No concussion. But he can't play football for three days."

Lucy laughed. "I'll bet that went over real well."

"Yeah, he's even more pissed at me now. I'm telling you, he scared the crap out of me. I've never seen him so mad."

"Forget about him. Tell me more about this Gavin guy. He sounds like a drop-dead hottie."

"He is." Just thinking about Gavin brought his image into Maya's head, his dark eyes burning with so much intensity he seemed to be looking right through her and into another dimension.

"So, spill already. What are you gonna do?"

"I don't know. It's like I'm living in a tornado. I thought my life would be so simple after I dumped Stuart. Now I've got two new guys asking me out and a psycho ex-boyfriend stalking me."

Lucy made a noise that was supposed to be a violin playing sad music, but which came out as a sort of spitting sound. Maya pictured pieces of popcorn hitting the phone. Lucy was many things, but demure would never be one of them. "Oh, poor baby. Boo hoo. So many men she doesn't know what to do. It's simple, sweetie. You see both of them. You're sixteen, you don't need to be tied to one guy. You've been there, done that. Now's the time to live a little."

"I'm not like you, Lucy. I can't bounce between guys."

"And, you don't bounce *on* them, either," Lucy said, not the least offended by Maya's comment. "That's even worse. You need to lighten up, girl. The way I see it, you've only got one real problem here."

"One? I can think of a dozen. Which one are you talking about?"

"Who you gonna ask to the dance, Blake or Gavin?"

Long after she hung up with Lucy, Maya still couldn't answer that question.

Chapter 11

On Monday, Lucy refused to drop the subject of Maya and her romantic problems. Since Maya couldn't get her relationship issues, or lack of them, out of her head anyhow, Lucy's one-track mind didn't get on her nerves as much as it normally might have.

"The worst part is, I can't get in touch with either of them," Maya said, as she and Lucy sat down to eat lunch. Monday meant meatloaf with instant mashed potatoes, so they'd both opted for salads.

"Why not?"

"Blake doesn't have a cell phone, and I...I can't call him at his house. And I forgot to get Gavin's number, or give him mine. It's like I turn into a complete dork around both of them."

"Practice makes perfect," Lucy mumbled around a mouthful of salad. After swallowing, she continued. "It's like learning to drive a car. You've got to remember to look in the mirror, use the blinkers, and work the pedals. But pretty soon you've got that baby rockin' and rollin' like a superstar."

"Are you talking about cars or sex?"

Lucy raised one eyebrow. "Dude. If I were talking about sex, I'd use better metaphors than blinkers and pedals. Nastier, too. It doesn't matter anyhow. You don't have to worry about either one of them. You'll see them sooner or later, and my guess is sooner."

Maya frowned. "How do you know that?"

"Because, silly, they both know where you work, and Blake knows where you live. You just better hope they don't show up at the same time!"

Until then, the possibility hadn't even occurred to her. But once in her head, it refused to go away.

For the rest of the afternoon, Maya kept her mental fingers crossed.

* * *

"Focus, Maya!"

Maya clenched her teeth and nodded at Master Spiegel. As much as she wanted to tell him to stop picking on her, she knew she wasn't bringing her A-game to the mat, as her father liked to say. The praise Spiegel had given her for successfully defending herself had rapidly devolved into, first, annoyance, and then barely-hidden frustration as she constantly missed her marks and was late blocking strikes from her opponents. The sting of being hit on the face and chest only compounded her aggravation further.

So, it was a relief to both of them when the class ended, and she was able to head to the locker room to change.

"Maya."

She stopped when Spiegel called her name, too embarrassed with her performance to even turn and look at her instructor.

"It's obvious something's on your mind. My suggestion is to go home and do some intense meditation. Clear your head and, then, you'll be able to think about whatever's troubling you without your emotions getting in the way."

Keeping her back to him, she nodded again. "Yes, Master Spiegel."

Like that's gonna help. My emotions are what's troubling me. As in, I'm attracted to two guys, and I have no freakin' idea what's the right thing to do.

In the locker room, she changed back into her street clothes, wishing for the millionth time the dojo had showers. She hated putting on clean clothes after sweating like a pig for forty-five minutes. She always made sure to go right home after her class, not even stopping for a soda anywhere. It was tough enough as a girl in a small town to compete with people like Mary Ellen Gordon, who somehow always looked picture-perfect, even after gym class. She had no desire to get spotted walking through town looking - and smelling - like she'd just run a marathon.

So she was relieved when she got home without seeing anyone she knew. Looking forward to a long, cool shower followed by a giant glass of ice tea, Maya was digging through her purse for her keys as she approached the porch, and never noticed the figure standing there until he spoke.

"Hello, Maya."

Maya's heart did a fast dance, and she dropped her keys as she looked up.

Gavin! But how did he know where I lived?

Her brain answered even as her mouth managed to stammer out a weak hello.

Hello, brain dead much? All he had to do was look up the address in the phone book.

The idea that he might have followed her never even crossed her mind.

"I hope it's all right that I waited for you here. No one answered when I knocked."

"Um, yeah, it's cool." Startled and mortified and slightly turned on all at once, Maya bent down and grabbed her keys, her eyes never leaving Gavin. He looked dangerously out of place on her porch, in his black pants, frilly white shirt, thigh-length black coat, and tall black leather boots. With his pale complexion and raven hair, he had an almost Goth look that went enticingly well with his 'I-don't-give-a-damn' attitude. Even from ten feet away, he caused funny feelings in her stomach, what Grandma Crompton always called butterflies.

She wondered how he could look so cool, not a single hair out of place or a drop of sweat on him, dressed in such heavy clothes, while she felt like a potato roasting in the oven, thanks to the overly-warm afternoon.

That reminded her of her own sweaty, sticky body. *Oh, God, I probably smell like old gym socks. I wonder if I can get past him fast enough so that I don't repulse him too much.*

Keeping her arms tight against her sides, Maya hugged the railing and post as she edged by Gavin, who just stood there, not moving closer - *thank God!* - but not giving an inch, either. One corner of his mouth tipped up in a slightly sardonic fashion, as if he were aware of her discomfort and considered it humorous.

Maya unlocked the door and stepped inside, immensely grateful for the cool air conditioning washing over her body and drying the perspiration. "C'mon in," she said, giving him a wave, and then found he was already inside, his crow eyes flitting back and forth, taking in every detail of the living room.

Although all she wanted to do was run upstairs and get in the shower, Maya forced herself to play the good hostess. "Do you want something to eat or drink? We've got ice tea, soda, water, and I know there's chips and crackers. Maybe cookies, too. My parents are always bringing the leftover desserts home from the diner."

Gavin turned his eyes to her and shook his head. "You're all I need right now."

Maya's stomach did a double flip and her mouth opened, but no words came out. How did someone respond to that? She knew what Lucy would do - strip off her top and jump into the guy's arms. But as much as her whole body screamed at her to do just that, her brain shouted no, and kept her frozen in place, watching as Gavin slowly walked through the room, brushing his fingers across different things. When he reached the digital picture frame on the end table, he stopped and stared at it for at least a minute before continuing his erratic circuit of the room, gradually moving back towards her.

Maya managed to find her tongue as Gavin stopped less than a hand's width away from her. A shiver ran across her body, and she wondered why the air conditioning was set so cold. "Um, I guess if you don't want anything you can watch TV down here while I go shower, and then we can--"

She stopped when Gavin pressed a chilly finger against her lips - *Geez, he's freezing, too. I gotta turn the AC down* - and gave her another of his sexy smiles.

"Hush. This is not the time to talk." He removed his finger and replaced it with his own lips, pushing them against hers while at the same time gripping her with one strong hand and pulling her close to him.

All thoughts of telling him 'no' crumbled to dust, and she gave in to the kiss, wrapping her arms around his waist and eagerly meeting his exploring tongue with hers.

What are you doing? her mind screamed, while another part, the lonely, sad-for-too-long part, shouted back, *Shut up! It's about time we enjoyed ourselves.*

All too soon, Gavin broke the kiss and leaned back just far enough so that they could look at each other. "Show me your room. Now."

Don't do it! For a moment, Maya hesitated. Bringing Gavin to her room was probably the worst thing she could do. She had a feeling her willpower might not be strong enough to keep her from going all the way if he guided her in that direction. Which he certainly seemed ready to do. And while her body cried out to give in, she didn't want to make a mistake and lose her virginity to someone who might not be around for very long.

Yet she found herself nodding, taking him by the hand, and leading him up the stairs, her body winning the perpetual struggle against her brain for once.

It'll be okay, she told herself*. I'll just make sure we don't go too far. After all, it's not like you've never been with a guy before. Just know your limits, and make him respect them.*

She repeated the mantra in her head as they entered her room and she shut the door. However, the moment the lock clicked, Gavin took control and pulled her to the bed, sitting them both down. He leaned into her and kissed her again, harder this time, almost painfully. His fingers dug into her arms, and she hoped there wouldn't be bruises later. His tongue danced with hers, and she found herself amazed that she'd ever thought Stuart or any of the other boys she'd dated were good kissers. Gavin brought passion and energy to each tiny movement, and she couldn't help but respond in the same fashion.

He pushed her back against the pillows, while at the same time one of his hands slid from her arm to her chest. She felt her whole body respond in ways that she'd never known before.

Had he continued to take his time, things might have been different. But without warning, he sat up and grabbed the waistband of her shorts, pulling them down to her knees in one swift motion.

That broke the spell.

"Stop it!" Maya clamped her legs together and pulled her knees up, blocking him from reaching for her underwear.

"You don't want me to stop, Maya," he said, forcing his hand between her legs.

"Wanna bet?" She kicked out with both feet, knocking him onto the floor.

He got to his knees and placed his hands on the bed, looking like a lion ready to pounce. Maya yanked her shorts up and pushed herself as far from him as she could get, until her back pressed against the headboard. She reached towards her nightstand then cursed her own stupidity for leaving her purse, with her cell phone in it, downstairs.

"I think you need to get the hell out of here," she said, fear doing an excellent job of dampening her libido.

He smiled, and Maya was surprised to see there was no anger in his expression, only amusement. "I'm sorry, I thought you were ready to experience true pleasure. In the future, I'll be sure to...control...my advances. I'll see you again, Maya. Very soon. Perhaps then you'll be more receptive."

Gavin stood up, and Maya wrapped her arms around her legs, afraid he might make another attempt. Instead, he opened the door, nodded to her, and walked out of the room.

Even through her anger and worry, Maya's body betrayed her with a pleasure-filled shiver at the thought of seeing Gavin again, of feeling his lips against hers.

"Great. You're getting hot and bothered by a psycho. If date rape was all you wanted, you could have stayed with Stuart." The sound of her voice quelled her anxiety. So a guy tried to go further than she'd wanted. What girl hadn't experienced that before? At least she had a good story to tell Lucy. Too bad she wouldn't be home from work for another couple of hours.

That leaves me with nothing but homework.

She got up from the bed and was ready to go downstairs to get something to eat when she realized something was wrong.

I never heard the front door close.

Suddenly her fear rushed back in full force. What if Gavin wasn't just another horny teenager who let his hormones get the better of him? Sure, he'd eventually stopped his advances. He had, in fact, done nothing worse than what dozens of guys in her class probably tried every Saturday night after a few beers.

But what if it were an act? What if he was waiting for her downstairs right now, planning something a lot worse for her than an unwanted feel? Thoughts of sexual assault, of all the news stories about girls disappearing, swirled through her head, and her legs threatened to buckle. Using the bed for support, she moved across the room to her window. Parting the curtains just enough to peer through, she looked down at her front yard.

Gavin stood in the center of her driveway, staring up at her, as if he'd known all along that his silence would terrify her into looking for him. And although she'd thought herself hidden, he raised one hand in a mocking salute. Maya let the curtain fall back in place, not wanting to give him the satisfaction of knowing he'd gotten to her. She counted to ten before looking once more.

This time the driveway was empty.

"Damn him!" She kicked a shoebox across the room. She didn't know whether to scream, cry, or laugh.

No, Gavin probably wasn't a rapist, but he sure was an asshole. He had to know that he'd scared her, and still he'd gone and purposely done something to piss her off. *Again.* Twice in five minutes. Even Stuart hadn't managed that.

Wait until Lucy hears about this.

Maya went downstairs, but before grabbing her phone she circled through the house and made sure all the doors and windows were locked. Only then did she relax enough to get a snack and return to her room.

Even so, she found herself unable to concentrate on her homework. Time dragged on in slow motion until it was time to call Lucy.

"Hey, chica, what's up?"

Just hearing her friend's voice made Maya feel better. "Um, I was wondering if you could come over for a while. Gavin was here earlier, and he turned out to be a Class-A douche. I need someone to eat junk food with me and tell me I'm not being paranoid."

"I'll be there faster than you can say 'Doritos.'"

"Make it faster."

Maya hit the 'end' button and sighed.

Ten minutes never seemed so long.

* * *

Gavin strode into the long exhibit room with a swagger, a self-satisfied smile on his aristocratic face.

Blake immediately knew something was wrong. Anything that pleased Gavin had to mean bad news for someone else. Possibly the whole town.

Down where Blake's stomach used to reside, a cold, sick feeling took form. Since they hadn't located the key yet, there was only one other thing that could make Coronado Bay's resident practitioner of the dark arts so happy.

Maya.

Blake prayed he was wrong, but the moment Gavin started speaking, he confirmed Blake's worst fears.

"Blake. So good to see you. Saves me the trouble of looking for you."

Gavin's men all stopped what they were doing and turned to look at the evil being who'd doomed them all to Hell. Anton Childs, who seemed to know what was going on, put a hand over his mouth to cover a laugh.

Knowing he couldn't avoid the confrontation, Blake faced Gavin from across the room. "What do you want?"

If possible, Gavin's smile grew wider. And crueler. "Just to chat, that's all. Seems like we have something in common. I believe her name is Maya, and her kisses are oh, so sweet and tasty, like a fresh piece of fruit. But then, you wouldn't know that yet, would you?"

Hatred swirled through Blake, creating a feeling similar to all the blood rushing to his face. He clenched his fists and took a step forward, but immediately two of Gavin's men grabbed hold of his arms.

"If you've hurt her, I'll kill you," Blake said, wishing he could make it true.

Gavin laughed. "Hurt her? Far from it. We had a date. She invited me up to her room, and we spent some time on her bed, getting to know each other better. She's a feisty one, but soft in all the right places." He made an hourglass motion with his hands for the benefit of the sailors and a couple of them whistled appreciatively, which only increased Blake's ire.

"You stay the hell away from her."

"Now, that wouldn't be right. Considering we've got another date planned very soon."

"Sir, didja take her blood? Did it work?"

With a snarl, Gavin turned on the man who'd spoken, his expression morphing from smug arrogance to furious anger. "You idiot. Do you think I'd be standing here like a fool if I'd blooded the bitch?"

Relief surged through Blake. *Thank God!* But how long could Maya hold out? It would be one thing to remain a virgin in the company of oafs like that Stuart fellow. But someone like Gavin, who had a serpent's forked tongue and the ability to charm a spinster's savings from her purse? She wouldn't stand a chance against him.

Then another thought occurred to him.

"Does she know you're not human?"

Gavin froze, and Blake saw tendons and muscles bulging in the other man's jaw as he fought to control himself. *Odd how there is nothing substantial to us, yet we appear human to each other, down to our bodies mimicking every aspect of their solid forms.*

After several seconds of silence, Gavin let out a breath and favored Blake with an icy-cold stare. "I do not believe she is aware of my...current state," he said, each word coming out in measured fashion. "And I do not intend for her to find out."

Now it was Blake who found himself smiling. "Then perhaps I should make it clear to her exactly who, and what, she's dealing with." Before any of the others could move, he let his body pass through the wall behind him and hurried out of the building as fast as his spirit form allowed. He heard Gavin shouting for someone to go after him, but he ignored it.

This is my chance to make things right.

* * *

Gavin swore as Blake's form disappeared. Even a few seconds head start meant he'd be long gone before the Black Lady's crew could catch up to him. Still, he called out to the watching sailors, "Quickly! Two of you, get after him! Find him or I'll sell your souls to the Prince of Darkness."

Two men raced across the room and disappeared through the wall. The remaining sailors looked expectantly at Gavin.

"What now, sir?" asked Anton Childs. "We need the witch's blood if we're to ever get ourselves free of this place."

"I'm well aware of what we need, Mister Childs. But what would you have me do, knock the girl about the head and carry her here? We've no idea how this magik works. It might not last. Could very well be I deflower her only to find that by the time I return, the magik is gone. Then we're no better off than now."

"Aye, there's that." The old man scratched at his chin. "But so, that gets me to thinking. A few minutes is all we need. So p'raps there's another way."

Intrigued, Gavin momentarily forgot his concerns over Blake telling the spirit-talker the truth about him. "And what might that be?"

Anton chewed his lip before speaking. "Well, if what the legends say is true, and 'tis taking the virgin blood of the witch that makes a spirit whole again, then it just might be that something half as good might work half as well."

Gavin felt his frustration mounting again. "Speak English, you old fool."

"What I mean is what if it be a regular virgin? That part of it must mean something, else you could use any old witch."

A smile crossed Gavin's lips. "In other words, taking any girl's virginity might just make me solid for long enough to find the key."

Anton nodded. "Right, sir."

Gavin laughed. "Then by all means, let's find ourselves another virgin."

Chapter 12

Maya hated Tuesdays more than any other day of the week. Sundays were bad because there was school the next day, and other days could be bad depending on how much homework she got or how busy work was. But Tuesdays were always guaranteed to be the worst.

It started in the morning. She had to be at school an hour early because she was the treasurer for her class, and each Tuesday morning the class officers had a meeting before first period. Only through sheer will and a large double latte did she manage to stay awake.

Then there was work right after school. She couldn't be late or miss a day because Tuesday was the busiest weekday for the diner, thanks to its being bowling night and all the league teams coming in for early dinners or late snacks. By the time her shift ended at nine, all she wanted to do was go home and go to bed.

Except she couldn't because she still had all her homework to do.

So when she walked out of the diner, already in a fouler than foul mood, and found Stuart Newman waiting on the sidewalk, it was all she could do to keep from screaming.

"We need to talk," Stuart said, falling in step next to her.

Maya considered going back into the diner, but there were enough businesses still open, and enough people on the streets, that she felt the confrontation wouldn't get physical on his part. "God, not now, Stuart. I've had a real crappy day."

"Yeah? Well I've had a real crappy week. And it all involves you. And you're not going anywhere until we talk about it." As he finished talking, he grabbed her arm and pulled her to a halt.

"Ow! Let go." She tried to pull free, but he tightened his grip.

"Not until you tell me what's going on."

All the anger building up inside Maya for the past several days finally burst open. "You want to talk? Fine. Here's the deal. I dumped you because I was sick and tired of your jealousy, your juvenile behavior, and the way you treated me like a possession, not a person. For as long as I was with you, I couldn't even say hi to another guy without you freaking. You know how many friends I lost because of you? And contrary to what you think, I never once cheated on you although everyone told me I should. And then, when I finally meet a nice guy, a guy who's not two steps away from being a psycho stalker, you come along and try to beat the crap out of him. So do us both a favor and stay the hell out of my life!"

Even in the yellow glow of the streetlights, Maya saw Stuart's face take on the red hue that signaled he'd gone from angry to furious.

"When did you turn into such a bitch?" He gave her a hard shake. "When you met that other guy? How long were you seeing him? Did Lucy cover for you?"

I can't believe it. Even after telling him she hadn't cheated, he still didn't believe her. *How could I have ever liked such a jerk?*

"Stuart--"

"Shut the hell up. You talked. Now it's my turn." He shook her again, harder this time, and she cried out.

"Stop it! You're hurting me."

"I'll hurt you even more if--"

"I think you should let go of her."

Maya and Stuart both turned to see a tall young man in a black coat standing a few feet away.

"Gavin." Maya didn't know whether to be glad for the interruption or frightened. If someone had asked her right then which of them was more dangerous, she'd have been hard-pressed to pick one.

Stuart glanced at her and, then, back at Gavin. "You know this guy?"

Before Maya could speak, Gavin answered for her. "Maya and I are acquainted, yes."

"Acquainted?" Stuart let go of her arm, but if anything, he looked even angrier. "You're seeing him, too? What, Lucy finally turned you into a slut like her?"

Gavin grabbed Stuart by the shirt and slammed him into a nearby building. Although the husky football player outweighed Gavin by at least twenty pounds, the taller man had no trouble moving him across the sidewalk. "That's no way to talk to a respectable woman."

"I'll kick your ass, you stupid--"

The rest of Stuart's words disappeared in loud gasp as Gavin drove a fist into his belly. Stuart fell to his knees, his face still red but for a different reason, as he clutched his midsection and struggled to breathe.

"Gavin! You didn't have to hit him." Yet, even as she protested, Maya felt a twisted pleasure at seeing Stuart on the ground. And another pleasure as well, something warm and comforting that sent her whole body tingling.

"I will not apologize for protecting your honor, Maya. I could not let him treat you that way."

Maya looked at her arm, where a bruise had already formed, five perfect finger-shaped purple marks. "You know what? You shouldn't apologize. It's all right. In fact," she added, taking his hand, "it's better than all right. If I want to date someone, or more than one someone, is there anything wrong with that?"

"Not at all." Gavin led her away from Stuart, who'd stopped groaning but hadn't gotten to his feet. "A beautiful young girl like yourself shouldn't be serious with just one person. You need to meet people, experience different outlooks and personalities. Otherwise, how will you ever learn who you are and what you want out of life?"

The warm feeling expanded, and Maya realized what it represented: freedom. Freedom to date who she wanted, to be herself instead of belonging to someone else. Without guilt and without worrying about what everyone thought.

Is this how Lucy feels all the time? Is that why she's always so carefree and happy?

"You're right, dammit," she said. "I'm my own person, not anyone else's. Not Stuart's, not Blake's, and not--" She stopped, suddenly aware of what she'd been about to say.

The potential insult didn't bother Gavin, who smiled. "Not mine, either. Although I hope that doesn't preclude our seeing each other on occasion."

As much as she knew she should tell Gavin she wasn't interested, somewhere between her brain and her mouth the words changed. "I suppose that can be arranged. But I'm warning you," she added, pointing a finger at him, "No means no. I've had my share of pushy people, and I'm not looking for a wrestling match every time we see each other."

Gavin's smile grew wider, and he chuckled softly. "Agreed. I'll do my best to be a gentleman. It's just that your beauty makes it difficult."

"Yeah, right. Flattery will get you nowhere." Even as she said it, Maya knew her face had betrayed her, that she was blushing furiously.

Politely pretending not to notice, Gavin asked if she wanted to take a walk with him. "It's a beautiful evening, and hopefully the actions of the young man back there haven't spoiled it for you."

Maya shook her head, feeling a pang of regret as she did so. "Ordinarily, I'd say yes in a heartbeat. But I've got a ton of homework due tomorrow, and I really have to get home. Raincheck?"

For a moment, Gavin's smile hardened, and she caught a glimpse of the person who'd gotten out of control in her bedroom. Then his face cleared, and he shrugged. "My loss. Perhaps tomorrow. Have a good night, Maya." He took her hand and kissed it, his lips and fingers cool against her skin.

"Goodnight."

As he walked away, she almost lost her resolve and told him she'd changed her mind, but she clamped her mouth shut and let him disappear around the corner.

Standing in the gathering darkness, Stuart a block behind her and long forgotten, Maya whispered to herself.

"Oh, man. What am I doing?"

Two boyfriends? That could only lead to trouble.

But it felt so good!

Hidden in the darkness between two buildings, Gavin watched Maya walk down Main Street and eventually turn onto the road that led to her house. Only when she was long out of sight did he finally let his frustration boil over. White, orange, and red streams of electricity shot out from his body, making him look like a character from a movie struck by lightning. Light bulbs and neon signs exploded in the two stores closest to him, and out on Main Street a power line separated from a pole with a burst of sparks and a sound like a gun shot. A second later, half the stores on the block went dark.

Muttering a string of increasingly vile curses, Gavin strode past gawking pedestrians towards the library, his presence nothing more than a curiously cold breeze in the warm autumn air.

* * *

Stuart Newman wondered if he was going crazy or if he'd been hit on the head too many times in football practice. The past ten minutes had been the weirdest in his life. After getting sucker punched by Maya's newest boyfriend, he'd had to endure watching them walk off together while he struggled to catch his breath. Of course, it wasn't like he'd been forced to watch them, but he'd found himself unable to tear his eyes away, like the time he'd caught his sister and her boyfriend having sex in her bedroom. He hadn't wanted to watch then, either, but there'd been some kind of sick fascination holding him in place.

With each step she took, Maya seemed to be exiting his life a little more. He hadn't expected to feel sad, but there'd suddenly been tears in his eyes as he realized it was finally over.

So at first, he'd simply blamed those tears when it seemed that the guy walking with her was slowly turning invisible. He'd wiped a hand across his face, clearing his blurry vision, but nothing changed.

The guy was disappearing!

Stuart squinted hard into the last remains of the dusk. As impossible as it might be, the guy was walking away from Maya, and at the same time he was fading away into thin air. Maya, a stupid, smitten look on her face, didn't even seem to notice. She'd just waited 'til he disappeared completely, and then headed down the street toward her house.

As if that wasn't strange enough, a couple of minutes later, while Stuart was still trying to process what he'd seen, a series of sparks shot out from the alley where the guy disappeared, and then all hell broke loose as a power line burst on Main Street and all the buildings went dark.

While people from the stores *oohed* and *ahhed* over the mysterious blackout, Stuart found himself unable to shake the feeling that the miniature lightning storm and Maya's disappearing boyfriend were somehow related.

The question was, how?

And what should he do about it?

Chapter 13

"Lucy, I'm telling you, he just appeared like some kind of dark prince to save the day. If Gavin hadn't been there, I don't know what Stuart would have done to me."

Maya's homework sat unopened on her desk, as it had for the past hour. She knew it meant another late night of hitting the books, but really, who could expect her to concentrate on her schoolwork after what happened? She'd been too tense, too worked up, and too excited to even think about history or science. So instead, she'd grabbed a handful of cookies and run upstairs to call Lucy. Texting was out of the question - she'd end up with carpal tunnel before finishing her story. Maybe once she talked everything out, got it out of her system, she'd be able to concentrate.

Maybe.

So far, that theory hadn't worked. Lucy kept asking for more details, and Maya found herself reliving Stuart's quasi-attack and Gavin's sexy rescue over and over.

"I can't believe you didn't let him walk you home," Lucy said, her voice equal parts teasing recrimination and envy.

"Yeah, right. After what happened the last time? I think it'll be awhile before I spend any time alone with Mister Grabby Hands, no matter how hot he...he is," she finished lamely.

Lucy didn't miss her hesitation. "How hot he is, or how hot he makes you?"

Maya didn't answer. She didn't want to admit the truth of it, to herself or Lucy.

"What's the matter, cat got your tongue? Or maybe you're thinking of where that tongue--"

"Okay, Lucy, that's enough. I gotta go. For real this time. Homework calls."

Maya punched the disconnect button on her cell, cutting Lucy off in mid-protest. Not that she'd be insulted. She got a kick out of seeing how far she could push Maya.

Probably spend half the night thinking of new ways to embarrass me tomorrow.

Normally the prospect of enduring Lucy's one-track teasing would have had Maya thinking of ways to avoid it - usually by giving her the silent treatment - but the way she felt at the moment, she could fail a pop quiz in every class tomorrow while the whole school made fun of her, without coming down from her cloud.

"Gotta concentrate," she whispered to the empty room. She flipped open her history book, but it only took a few seconds before the lines of text blurred and all she saw was Gavin's face and tall, lithe body. Already her imagination was changing the events of that evening. In her mind, Gavin emerged from a cloud of fog, his black coat whipping behind him with primal fury as he strode towards her, one side of his mouth tipped up in a sultry half-smile that begged to be kissed.

"Maya." Hearing her name from his lips sent chills down her back, and it took her a moment to realize she wasn't imagining it.

"Maya. May I come in?"

"Yes." The word was already leaving her mouth as she turned and saw Blake sitting on her windowsill.

He climbed in and stood up. "Maya, we need to talk. There's something--"

"Shut up." Maya didn't know which of them she surprised more by grabbing him and pressing her lips against his. For a moment he stood still as a statue, then his arms went around her, and he angled his face without breaking contact.

Maya shivered as the chill emanating from his lips, hands, and body covered her from three directions at once. Rather than putting out the fire raging inside her, it served as cold fuel, each tingling wave heightening the sensations she felt.

Still locked in their kiss, she pulled him towards her bed and let her body fall backwards onto the comforter, dragging him along with her. Stuffed animals and pillows toppled to the floor as they rolled back and forth, taking turns on top. His hands drew frigid trails down her back and sides and her palms felt like ice from holding tightly to him. She gasped when icy fingers crept under her shirt and bra, but didn't even think of telling Blake to stop.

Until two of those fingers opened the button of her shorts.

"Please, don't." Misty vapor formed as her breath flowed over Blake's otherworldly form.

"Don't fight it, Maya, it's for the best." His hand slid further down, and suddenly it was like a glass of cold water on her hormones.

"Dammit, I said no!" She pushed away from him, feeling an eerie déjà vu. What was it about her bed that turned nice guys into dogs? Was it always going to be like this?

"You need to have sex, Maya. Right away." Blake's expression was serious and clinical, as if he'd just told her she needed to take her vitamins every day and drink plenty of water.

"Oh, really? Well, I've got news for you. I decide what I need, and when I need it. And the last thing I want from you right now is sex."

Instead of being angry, Blake nodded. "Okay. It doesn't have to be me. It can be anyone. Your ex-boyfriend. Someone from school. Anyone except Gavin--"

"All right, that's enough. Get out." Maya couldn't believe it. Blake was jealous of Gavin! He must have seen the two of them together, maybe even earlier that night.

Oh, God, is that the only reason he came here?

"But Maya, you don't understand. Just let me--"

"I said out, Blake. Now. Scram. Make like an egg, and beat it." She leaned forward and pushed him, sent him flying off the bed. "I mean it. Get the hell out of my room."

This time he did look angry, but unlike Gavin the day before, he didn't press the issue. Instead, he went to the window and climbed out. As soon as he disappeared, Maya shut and locked it. She had no idea if a ghost could move through walls, but if nothing else, it would send a message that she didn't want him coming back.

Her hands trembled as she buttoned her shorts and straightened her shirt. She picked up her history book again but had even less success than before trying to concentrate.

Dammit to Hell!

The book hit the wall across the room, and Maya threw herself down on the bed, beat at the pillows and comforter with her fists until her arms ached. When she sat up, sweaty and flushed, instead of feeling better for having released her pent up frustrations, she felt more charged up than before if that were possible.

Maybe I should have...

No. That's just the hormones talking. You'll know when it's the right time. And, this wasn't it.

Unfortunately, knowing she'd done the right thing didn't make her feel any better.

Downstairs, a door slammed. Her mother, home from work.

I can't let her see me like this.

She grabbed her pajamas and ran for the bathroom, hoping a nice, cool shower would calm her down and clear her head.

If not, it's gonna be a long, long night.

Chapter 14

"Girl, you look like a reject from a bad zombie movie."

Maya didn't bother acknowledging Lucy's comment as the two friends took seats next to each other in homeroom. She knew exactly how bad she looked. She hadn't fallen asleep until well after three. She didn't even remember hitting the snooze button and going back to sleep when her alarm went off at six-fifteen. If her mother hadn't come in and woken her at twenty to seven, she'd probably still be in dreamland. As it was, she'd had just enough time to run a brush through her hair and throw some clothes on. Everything else would have to wait until after class.

Not one to accept silence, Lucy gave her a poke with the eraser end of her pencil. "What's the deal? Late night? Who was it, Gavin or Blake? Give me the juicy, girl."

Thinking about both boys made Maya groan. "Ugh. I don't want to talk about either of them right now. I overslept thanks to the two of them being jerks. Look at me. No makeup, no lipstick, not even any blush or cover-up. Geez, the boys'll be lining up to ask me to the dance now, huh?"

"All guys are jerks. But don't worry. We'll fix you up after first period. I always have my emergency make-up kit in my bag. Besides, it's not your face that's gonna keep the guys away."

Something in Lucy's voice caught Maya's attention, even through her fog of exhaustion. "What do you mean?"

"I was gonna tell you after class, but I guess I don't have to worry about ruining your morning now. It's Stuart."

Jerk number three. Naturally. "Oh, no. What's he done now?"

Lucy shook her head. Her black hair, cut in a bob this month, swished back and forth. "You're not gonna believe it. He's been spreading the word that if anyone asks you to the dance, he'll personally rearrange their body parts."

Maya felt her face tighten. "Tell me you're joking."

Behind her rose-colored eye shadow, Lucy's eyes held equal amounts of compassion and sympathetic outrage. "I wish. Oakley told me on the way to school. Seems your ex is mounting a major campaign to keep you boy-free for the foreseeable future."

"That son-of-a-"

"Class, please put your books under your desks, and take out your pencils and calculators. We're having a little quiz."

A chorus of groans followed Mr. Rollo's announcement. Lucy's was the loudest. "I can't believe it. A pop quiz in chemistry? Who does that?"

Maya put her head on the desk. "Could this day get any worse?"

* * *

Gavin Hamlin stood in a storeroom in the museum's basement, his attention focused on the young woman who was opening boxes with an odd triangular blade and sorting the contents on a long table. She'd caught his attention the moment she'd entered the building, thanks to the Virgin-a-Teens button pinned to her shirt. He'd followed her into the basement, a plan already forming in his mind for testing Anton's theory about virgin blood. After waiting several minutes to make sure no one would be joining her, he'd moved close to her, so close she'd shivered and rubbed her arms.

You think you're cold now, he thought, watching the gooseflesh rise on her skin. *Wait until I can really touch you.*

His plan was a simple one. He'd known for some time that unlike his fellow ghosts, he had the ability to actually affect what happened around him in the real world by causing episodes of electrical energy, usually fueled by intense emotion. Whether these derived from his own forceful personality or his years of practicing magik, he had no idea. But it was time to put them to good use.

Just as he would for a spell, he focused his concentration, putting all his effort into it, until it felt like his head would explode. He let his anger and frustration at being dead and denied his ultimate goal fuel him, build up inside him until it felt like he couldn't contain it any longer.

Just when he reached the point where his brain threatened to explode, he released the energy one massive surge, keeping his eyes on the girl's hands. The lights flickered momentarily, but better than that, one of her hands jerked as she opened a box.

The hand holding the small knife.

"Ow!" The girl held up her other hand. A tiny cut on her thumb bled a few ruby-red drops.

Yes! Gavin leaned forward, extended an incorporeal hand out, and touched his fingers to the droplets.

And felt the girl's warm skin.

Knowing his slight solidity wouldn't last long, he grabbed the knife from her. It passed partway through his hand, but not all the way. Lifting it, he swung it as fast as he could.

The girl never had time to scream as the blade sliced through her throat. Blood sprayed out onto Gavin's flesh, and he felt himself grow more solid. He brought his arm back, cutting deeper into the muscles and tendons of her neck. This time a fountain of blood exploded over him. Dropping the knife, he scooped handfuls of her blood and smeared it on himself, reveling in the hot, sticky liquid. In moments, he was nearly as solid as a living person.

Now, to find the key. Gavin grabbed the knife and ran up the stairs to the main floor. Even in his haste, he spared some of his attention to being physically part of the real world again. Colors seemed brighter; and when he took a deep breath, he was able to smell odors again - metal and dust and leather and a thousand other scents. The dead girl's blood was cold and tacky against his skin, and he loved it.

Although he'd been prepared to use the knife on anyone he saw, Gavin found the Black Lady's exhibit room empty. He immediately began searching through any items where a key might have been hidden, tossing the objects to the floor as he finished with them. As he raced against time, he grew more frustrated, throwing utensils and tools across the room and cursing Fate for sending the ship to the ocean's bottom in the first place.

He'd gone through the contents of an entire table when suddenly his hand passed through a broken jewelry box in the middle of picking it up.

"NO!" he cried, as the box tumbled to the table. "No! I'm not finished!"

All through the museum, light bulbs exploded as excess energy coursed through them. Thunder boomed over Coronado Bay and lightning flashed even though there were no clouds. In the buildings on either side of the museum, the power went out for several minutes.

Gavin's furious shrieking continued, but by then no humans could hear him.

Chapter 15

"But Mom, it's just for a couple of hours. I *have* to go." Maya hoped her inflection was just right, not too whiny, showing just the perfect amount of urgency.

"You don't *have* to do anything," Emily Blair said. "You can study at home. I don't want you running around town while there's a murderer on the loose."

Since its discovery earlier in the afternoon, the dead girl's body had been the primary topic of conversation at school and in town. She'd been a senior at Boston College, working part-time at the museum for an internship. Like all small towns, news in Coronado Bay traveled faster by mouth than by radio or TV, although media types from as far away as New York City had already converged on the museum, eager to tell the world the story of the "shocking murder in the small seaside village."

"I won't be running around town. I'll be at the library with Lucy. I have to do research for a school project."

"Tell Lucy to come here. You can check the books out or use the damn Internet for something other than games and gossip." Emily Blair's voice was edging towards finality, and Maya knew she only had one more chance to change her mother's mind.

"We can't, Mom. The books we need are reference books, and you can't check them out of the library."

Mrs. Blair's eyes narrowed. Maya held her breath. After what seemed like forever, her mother sighed; Maya knew she'd won.

"Fine. But I will drive you there myself. And, when you're done, you go straight from the library to the diner."

"I promise!" Maya gave her mother a quick kiss and ran upstairs to call Lucy before her mother could change her mind.

* * *

"I can't believe you talked me into this." Lucy Patton stared at the pile of books on the table and grimaced. "You *know* Thursday nights are for *Beverly Hills Cheerleader* and *Vampire Princess*."

"You'll be home in plenty of time to see them," Maya said, flipping pages in one of the massive books. She was searching for any information she could find about the Black Lady and its disastrous trip. It would have been easier just to go back to the museum, but they'd closed the place indefinitely because of the murder. Besides, she had no desire for Blake to find her researching his history.

"I better be. Everyone at school's gonna be talking about them tomorrow; if I haven't seen them, I'll be *sooo* pissed."

"You have my word. We'll be out of here before seven." Maya closed the book and grabbed another. She purposely didn't mention that the library closed at seven. "Sooner, if you start helping me."

"The things I do for you." Lucy opened a book and started reading.

Once Lucy stopped complaining, Maya lost track of time as she read through one tome after another, seeking out any mention of the Black Lady. Most of the books were historical treatises about New England's shipping industry, but a few were actual port logs, containing manifest records and details of ships leaving and entering Coronado Bay's harbor.

Around them, the library was a vast cave perpetually cloaked in twilight, the only sounds the muted echoes of whispered voices or soft footsteps. Once, someone several racks away dropped a book to the floor, and Maya jumped in her seat.

"This place is totally creepy," Lucy said, even her usual animated personality muted by the oppressive atmosphere.

"Mmm-hmm." Maya barely heard her. She'd caught the words Black Lady as she skimmed pages. The mention turned out to be a list of port entries from Manhattan, dated 1908.

"Lucy! Look at this!"

Someone shushed her from a nearby table, and Maya lowered her voice. "This is it. The Black Lady. Left Manhattan in 1908, heading for Boston. It's the ship's manifest, I think."

"What'd they have? Gold? Jewels?" Lucy leaned forward, a hint of interest on her face.

"I haven't found that yet. But here's the crew. And the captain, Jonas Freeman. And passengers. Oh, crap. Look." Maya pointed to a name.

"Gavin Hamlin of Boston Towne? Isn't that the name of the guy you met? Some coincidence."

"Yeah." Maya's stomach turned over as the significance of finding Gavin's name struck her.

The clothes. The formal way he acted.

His cold hands.

Oh, crap. I'm an idiot. He's a ghost, just like Blake. They were on the boat together, even if Blake's name isn't on the manifest. That means they know each other.

"Maybe he's a relative," Lucy said. "That's why he's doing research at the museum. You should ask him next time you see him."

"I'll do that." Maya stood up. "I'm going to make photocopies of these entries. Be right back."

The copy machine was sequestered in a small alcove away from the main reading room, so as not to disturb anyone. On her way there, she noticed all the other patrons had left, leaving her and Lucy alone. As Maya walked down the aisle, a book fell over on one of the shelves with a soft thump, and her heart jumped a beat in response. All of a sudden, the library didn't seem so safe. Just the opposite, in fact. The lights seemed too murky, and the shadows too sinister. The murder at the museum fresh in her memory, Maya quickened her pace, but the click-clack of her heels on the granite floor only added to the nervous feeling growing in her chest.

An overhead light flickered, sending the aisle into momentary darkness. In that brief second, a chill breeze brushed across her back. Goosebumps sprouted on her arms. She emerged from the aisle and welcomed the slightly brighter glow emanating from the copier alcove ahead of her.

Thirty feet, she told herself. *Nothing can happen in thirty feet.*

But that wasn't true, was it? All sorts of things could happen, especially in a dark, empty room filled with hiding places. Against her will, her thoughts returned to the girl at the museum. She'd been alone in a room, too, and someone had slit her throat. Then her killer had walked down the hall and up the stairs, leaving a trail of blood the whole time, as if he didn't care in the least about getting caught.

Up the stairs and into the Black Lady exhibit.

That's where they'd found the last of the footprints and handprints. Whoever had killed the poor girl had trashed the exhibit and then escaped without being seen.

As if he'd disappeared.

Like a ghost.

More cold air washed over her, and she wrapped her arms around herself, clutching the heavy book to her chest. Halfway to the alcove. With each step, her mind continued down lines of thought she didn't want to consider.

Why didn't I notice he was a ghost?

Because you were so moon-eyed over him you wouldn't have noticed if he carried a butcher knife and had a white hockey mask hanging from his belt.

Was he the killer? He did have a temper.

So does Blake. Could he be the killer?

How well do they know each other? Could they be in on it together?

How could either of them have done it? They can only be solid around me.

Of course, how do I know that's true? I only knew one ghost before this. Maybe they're all different.

Five steps away. Three. The idea of reaching the alcove seemed like the most important thing in the world.

Two.

"Maya."

She gasped at the sound of someone speaking her name, then realized it was only Lucy.

"Oh, hell, you scared the crap out of me."

"Yeah." Lucy smiled. "Gotcha. Told you this place is major creepy. I stuck the other books on a returns cart. Let's make your copies and get out of here. You can treat me to a piece of pie before you start your shift."

Maya dropped a quarter into the machine with a shaking hand.

"You've got a deal."

* * *

Several aisles away, Gavin Hamlin stood in the shadows, watching as Maya and her friend finished what they were doing and headed for the front of the library. Although he'd been afraid to approach too close, lest Maya's ability make him visible to her, he'd managed to catch part of their conversation, enough to know they'd discovered something about the Black Lady.

"Why didn'cha just kill her?" Anton asked from behind him. All the remaining sailors from the Black Lady had gathered with him, in the hope that Gavin would find a way to slice the girl open and use her blood to set them free.

"I need a weapon, something to make her bleed."

"You could have dropped books on her noggin' 'til she bled."

He shook his head. "Her friend was too close. She would have seen."

"We could have killed them both."

Gavin turned to Anton, his dark eyes colder than the ocean depths. "You idiot. It's only Maya who gives us shape and weight. To the other you'd be nothing but cold air. She would have had plenty of time to escape before we drew any blood."

He gave them time to realize the logic of his words then continued. "When the time is right, when she is alone, that is when I will take her life."

"You'd best do it soon. The deadline approaches."

"I'm well aware of the deadline, Mister Childs. Over a hundred years I've waited. I won't let this opportunity pass. I will kill the girl.

"And her blood will be mine."

* * *

Thanks to the murder, business was slow at the diner - for a Thursday night, at least. The majority of the regulars showed up, mostly single men and women and older couples who preferred eating out to staying home alone, all of them going on and on about the killing, picking at each tiny detail like crows feasting on a highway carcass, until there was nothing left. Then, as people in a small town are wont to do, they began adding their own details, until a casual listener might have been excused for thinking a full-scale massacre had occurred.

But not many families came in, and those that did ate quickly and hurried home. By the time nine o'clock rolled around, only a handful of people remained seated at the counter, and all the tables and booths were empty. Maya's father told her she could go home early, as long as Manny Esposito, a heavily-muscled teenager who doubled as a dishwasher and kitchen assistant, walked her home. Eager to leave, Maya accepted without an argument.

Once she was safely locked in the house and had called her parents to let them know, she poured herself a glass of ice tea and brought it to her room where she opened her laptop.

And yelped in surprise when she saw a face reflected in the screen.

Turning, she found Gavin Hamlin standing by her closet door, looking as cruelly handsome as ever. He wore the same clothes as before, only now Maya understood why. As a ghost, he could never change them.

"Hello, Maya. I am sorry for startling you. But I had to see you again."

He stepped into the meager light from her desk lamp, and as it illuminated him better, Maya felt a small measure of relief when she saw his clothes were free of any blood stains. No one could have killed that woman without getting tons of blood on them. That, along with the fact that she had never heard of anyone besides herself who could make ghosts solid, convinced her Gavin couldn't have done it.

It has nothing to do with how hot he looks.

She chose to ignore that last thought.

"It's not nice to break into people's houses." She tried to put some anger into her voice, but even she could hear how weak it sounded.

His smile grew wider, more arrogant, and she knew he'd seen through her pretense, as well. "I didn't break in."

"Right. You drifted in, or floated, or passed through the window. Whatever it is you ghosts do."

Maya took some pleasure in seeing Gavin's self-confident grin fall away. She had a feeling he was a hard person to surprise.

"What? How did--"

"How did I know? I saw your name on the Black Lady's passenger list. I should have guessed sooner, from the clothes and the way you talk."

He sat down on her bed, eyeing her in a new way. Almost as if he was really seeing her for the first time.

"And this doesn't frighten you?"

Now it was Maya's turn to smile. "Why should it? I've known all my life that I can see ghosts, that the closer they are to me the more solid they become. That I can talk to them, even feel them. So, how many of you are there?"

"Ghosts?"

She laughed. "No, silly. People from the Black Lady. How many of you are hanging around the museum?" A sudden thought struck her. "Were you there when the girl got killed? Did you see who did it?"

A strange expression crossed Gavin's aristocratic face and then was gone in an instant. He shook his head. "Sadly, I did not see the events that took place this afternoon. I was...exploring the town. I spend much of my time doing that, since there is so little else to occupy my days and nights. When I returned to the museum, the police had already taken the body away."

"You make it sound like you hate being at the museum."

"I don't enjoy being around reminders of my own death."

"Oh. I hadn't thought about it that way." Maya found herself moving toward him before she even considered what she was doing. As if it were her body, not her mind, that decided to get up and sit next to Gavin on the bed.

"Your body is smarter than you," she imagined Lucy telling her.

Maya placed her hand on Gavin's, felt a chill run through her at the feel of his cold flesh, a chill that quickly turned to quivers of excitement as he leaned forward and kissed her. It was like kissing someone on a cold winter night, or after sucking on an ice cube, except that the other person's lips never warmed up. She moved closer and his arms went around her. His tongue met hers, ice to her fire, and she marveled at how different his kisses were than Blake's or Stuart's. Forceful and confident, just like his personality, as if he knew he was good at what he was doing. Was proud of it.

Maybe Lucy's right. I should date more people. Does everyone kiss differently? Are there people out there who are better at it than even Gavin or Blake? Or is it the thrill of kissing someone not human that I get off on?

Before she could ponder the answer to her last thought, Gavin's hand slipped beneath her shirt, his palm icy against the flesh of her stomach. She twitched slightly, but didn't break the kiss.

Why shouldn't she do it? What was the point of holding out when everyone said it felt so good?

"You go, girl!" Lucy's voice in her mind again, and this time Maya agreed.

Breaking the kiss and the embrace, Maya pulled her shirt off and lay back on the bed. Gavin's face loomed over hers, the expression she once thought harsh and cold now nothing but seductive. His kisses moved from her lips to her neck, and then down to the small triangle of skin between neck and breasts. It reminded her of running an ice cube over her flesh on a hot day. A soft moan escaped her lips as one of his hands came up and squeezed her, his coolness seeping through the thin material of her bra.

"I've wanted this for so long," he whispered in her ear. Each word was an autumn breeze against her flesh.

"So have I," she said. She reached back to unclasp her bra.

And then she screamed as the house went crazy around her. Lights flashed on and off, the house phone and her cell phone rang simultaneously, and the house alarm system triggered, filling the air with its strident howl. On her desk, her small flat screen TV came alive.

Maya pushed out from under Gavin and jumped off the bed. "What the hell's going on?"

Before Gavin could answer, the noise stopped and the lights came back on.

"What the...?"

Gavin reached out and took hold of her hand. "Everything is normal again. Come back to me."

"Are you crazy?" Fear had totally banished Maya's lust. "I have to call my parents. Either something's wrong with the wiring or someone tried to break into the house."

Gavin tugged at her arm but Maya pulled harder, breaking his hold. "This is not the time. I am seriously freaked. You better leave." She picked up her cell and hit the number for the diner. Then, seeing the look on Gavin's face, she quickly said, "Come see me tomorrow, okay?"

He nodded and, then, stepped out the window, just as her mother answered the phone.

"Mom? Something really weird just happened here. I think you better tell Dad to come home."

* * *

From behind a large tree in the neighboring yard, Blake Hennessy watched as Gavin's spirit floated out of Maya's window and headed back towards town. Had he still been corporeal, Blake would have fallen to the ground, his legs too weak to hold him up. As it was, he barely had enough strength to fight the pull of the Black Lady, which wanted to yank him back to the museum. He'd used every bit of energy he had to cause the electrical commotion in Maya's house, but it had been well worth it. Not only had he stopped Gavin from taking Maya's virginity, but he'd learned that he, too, could control the spirit energies the same way Gavin did, if not as powerfully.

Not yet, anyway. But I will. I have to, if I want to keep Maya safe.

He waited and watched until Maya's father came home, then slowly headed down the road that led to the beach.

Chapter 16

Friday

Maya leaned against a bank of lockers while Lucy pulled out her books for first period. Around them, students moved up and down the jam-packed hallway like blood cells in arteries and veins. "I'm telling you, it was freaky. I nearly peed in my pants. The whole house went crazy."

Lucy shut her locker. "I can't believe you didn't hop back into bed."

"Um, hello, scared out of my wits? It was kind of a buzz kill." Maya hoisted her book bag. "But I think I might've...you know..."

"Banged him?" Lucy gave her a devilish grin. "Bopped his socks off? Lap danced his--"

"I was going to say 'gone all the way,' but I should've known you'd have a more colorful way of putting things."

"So things were hot and heavy? That's cool, but it brings up a question."

"What's that?" Maya asked, taking her seat in chemistry.

"What about Blake?"

"I don't know. Blake's nice. Sweet. But Gavin is..."

"Hot?"

"Yeah. Majorly hot."

Lucy took a tube of lip gloss from her purse, puckered, and applied a shiny coating. "So, what's the verdict?"

"What do you mean?"

"Date one or date them both?"

"Both?" Maya gave a short laugh. "I'm not sure I'm ready for that. I have enough problems when I date one person. I can't imagine dating two at the same time."

"Anyone else, I'd disagree, but with you, I see your point. You gonna ask him to the dance?"

Just then the bell rang, saving Maya from trying to give an answer she didn't have.

* * *

Although Maya pondered Lucy's question all day, she still wasn't any closer to an answer when she got home from school. Finding Blake sitting on her porch didn't improve her mood.

"I told you to stop spying on me," Maya said, pushing past his chilly presence.

"We need to talk." He followed her into the house, and she found herself wishing ghosts were like vampires, that they needed an invitation to enter.

"So talk." She dropped her book bag on the couch and grabbed a soda from the fridge.

"It's, um, about your needing to lose your virginity." Somehow, although he didn't have any blood, Blake's face still turned pink from embarrassment. Even as she took out her pent-up frustrations on him, Maya wondered if his blushing were possible because he gained solidity in her presence.

"I really wish to Hell that you and everyone else would just mind your own business when it comes to my virginity!" The fact that she'd been ready to give it up the night before, could still feel Gavin's hands on her skin, didn't help. She felt her own face growing hot and not just from the awkwardness of the situation. Her hormones had been in an uproar all day, especially whenever thoughts of Gavin entered her head.

"You don't understand--"

"No, *you* don't understand!" Maya pointed a finger at him. "It's my body, and I'll do whatever, and whoever, I want with it. Got it?"

"Maya, please listen--"

"We are so done here." She took her soda and headed for the stairs.

Until Blake's next words stopped her in mid-step.

"Gavin Hamlin is planning on taking your blood and becoming solid again, forever, and then he's going to rape you and kill you."

A chill ran through Maya, colder than anything caused by a ghost. Slowly, she turned to face Blake. "Is this some kind of sick joke?"

His face told her it wasn't. Semi-solid because of the distance between them, he softly slumped onto the couch and shook his head. "I wish it were. Sit down. I'll explain everything or at least try to."

Maya came back down the stairs and took a seat on a chair across from Blake.

And, she felt an awful terror come to life inside her as he told the true story of the Black Lady and the sorcerer Gavin Hamlin.

* * *

Fifteen minutes later, Blake leaned back, his face showing how miserable he felt. "And that's why I had to...to try and do...you know. Before Gavin."

Maya stared at him, trying to make sense of everything he'd just told her. Gavin, the last of a long line of evil magicians. Blake, descended from a family that had vowed to wipe out the Hamlin lineage. He didn't seem crazy - *although how can you tell with a ghost?* So she had to figure he believed there was truth to what he'd said.

Besides, why make up such an elaborate lie? There were easier ways to get into a girl's pants.

Through the mass of thoughts swirling through her head, an idea came to her. "But I'm not a witch. So my blood is useless to him."

He shrugged. "It's a matter of definition. You have the ability to make us solid again. In my time, that's more than enough of a magical ability to be considered a witch. Besides, it doesn't matter what you are. It only matters what Gavin thinks you are, and what he's going to do."

"So why hasn't he tried to kill me yet?"

"He's been playing a game. He knows that I, well, that I like you, and he wants to, um, take your...um, what you don't want to talk about, before I do."

Maya's anger rose up again. "So I'm like, some kind of game for the two of you? Winner gets my virginity?"

"No!" Blake couldn't meet her gaze. "I only wanted to save your life."

"I thought you said you liked me." Maya wanted to bite her lip, but the petulant words were already out. *My hormones again. God, maybe Lucy's got the right idea. I'd be a lot less stressed if I were having sex.*

"I do. But I'd never force myself on a girl, on you. Except..."

"I know. Except to save my life." She sighed. It was all too much for her to handle. Things were much simpler before meeting either one of them. Which reminded her...

"Well, at least it solves one problem."

"What is that?" Blake asked.

She gave him a wry smile. "I don't have to worry about choosing between the two of you or trying to date both of you at once."

Blake's eyes went wide. "You mean you wanted to date me?"

Maya let her smile grow warmer. She should have known better than to get suckered by Gavin's dangerous looks and attitude. How many times had she warned Lucy to stay away from guys like that?

It was so flattering, though. That a dangerous guy might want me. Instead, all it did was blind me to the truth.

That the right guy was in front of me all along.

"I did," she told him. "And I still do. That is, if you don't hate me for the way I've acted."

His own smile slowly blossomed on his face, a morning sun rising out of dark clouds. "I'd like that a lot."

Maya found herself getting up and crossing the distance between them, sitting down next to him. As she moved closer, his form lost its translucence until she could no longer see through him. Like a ghost herself, standing outside her body as it did things on its own, she watched her hands take his. "There's a dance on Saturday night. Would you go with me?"

Oh my God, did I just ask him out? How can I bring him around other people, people I know and -

"Yes, I will."

Before she could think or say anything else, he leaned forward and placed his lips gently on hers. Her body responded, pressing close against his, pushing her mouth against his, savoring the cool caress of his ghostly flesh. He started to pull back, and she raised her hands to his neck, pulled his head forward, forcing the kiss to continue. His hands, now free, glided up her back, raising goosebumps and causing involuntary shivers that danced down to her stomach and lower, heightening her excitement further. She started to lean back, bringing him with her, when suddenly he broke the embrace and sat up straight.

"What's the matter?" Her breathing was heavy; she wanted nothing else except to have him on top of her again.

"You said Saturday night. The dance."

"Yeah? So what?" She tugged at his arm, but he didn't move.

"That's the deadline for Gavin to find the key and put his plan into action. If he's going to succeed, he has to kill you before midnight on Saturday."

Blake's words acted like a cold shower, dowsing the fire burning inside her. "Wait, there's a deadline? Why? And, what can we do to stop him?"

"I don't know." He shook his head in frustration. "I don't know where the book or key is. I don't know what kind of evil ceremony he has planned. I don't know anything!" He punched the couch pillows.

Once again, Maya found herself smiling.

"That's okay. I know just the person to talk to."

* * *

"Are you sure this will work?"

"Quiet!" Maya motioned for Blake to sit down. "Like I said, no guarantees, but I'm hoping." She closed her eyes and tried to block out all her other thoughts.

"Grandma, can you hear me? I need your help. Grandma Elsa, I need you. Grandma, this is--"

"I know who it is, silly girl. Who else would be calling me?"

"Grandma!" Maya ran forward and threw her arms around her grandmother, who returned the hug with equal gusto before stepping back and eyeing Blake.

"Well, you've certainly gotten yourself into quite a mess."

"You don't know the half of it. Grandma, this is Blake Hennessy. Blake, this is my grandmother, Elsa Crompton."

Blake nodded to her. "Pleased to make your acquaintance, ma'am."

"Nice to meet you, too, Blake. At least this one has manners," Elsa added, glancing at Maya.

"He's a ghost."

Elsa rolled her eyes. "Yes, dear. I know. We can recognize our own. But I'm guessing he's not the reason you called for me."

"No. I've got a major problem."

Maya quickly explained the situation, with Blake adding an occasional point. When they were done, Maya regarded her grandmother, whose normally happy face was all tight lips and dark frowns.

"So, is it true? Can Gavin really, like, use my blood to come back to life?"

"I'm afraid so. But you have the details wrong. It's not the act of losing your virginity that brings about the effect. It's simply using a virgin's blood."

"You mean any virgin will do?" Blake asked. Elsa started to answer, but Maya interrupted as a sudden thought came to her.

"The girl at the museum!"

"What girl?" Grandma Elsa asked.

"That is why Gavin killed her," Blake said.

"Children..." Elsa's voice took on a warning tone Maya remembered from her childhood.

"Someone killed a girl at the museum. Her blood was all over the place. According to the papers, she was a member of the Virgin-i-teens."

"That means Gavin might already be alive again. We have to do something!" Blake stood up.

"No, it doesn't," Elsa said. "Not unless she had the same powers as Maya."

Blake looked relieved as he sat down again. "So, magic is necessary, as well?"

"Yes." Elsa looked at each of them. "The blood of a virgin will make a ghost whole again, but only for a few minutes. But the blood of a Seer--"

"What's a Seer?" Maya interrupted.

"You are. A Seer is someone who can see the spirits of the departed. A Seer's blood is special. It would bring a ghost back to this world permanently."

"Why didn't you ever tell me about this before?" Maya asked. "I could have made you solid again." The idea of having her grandmother back, alive, around all the time, brought tears to her eyes.

"I would never think of it," Elsa said, crushing Maya's brief fantasy. "I don't want to hang around forever, like some undead thing from a horror movie. Besides, how would we explain my suddenly coming back to life after all these years?"

"And there is one other problem, as well." Blake's tone of voice let Maya know the problem would be a serious one.

"Yes." Elsa nodded. "We don't know how much blood is needed. It could take a lot, possibly so much that you would die."

"Oh." Maya found herself at a loss for further words. She loved her grandmother dearly. And she felt affection - maybe even something more - for Blake.

But was she ready to die so they could come back to life?

Shouldn't she be? She didn't think so, but the idea left a little guilt in its wake anyhow.

"Don't feel sad," Elsa said. "Immortality isn't all it's cracked up to be. Can you imagine being my age forever? Or," she added, glancing at Blake, "a teen-ager? Watching your friends, the people you love, grow old and die around you, while you never change?"

"I hadn't thought of it that way." Maya let out a sigh. "That still leaves us with the big problem. Gavin. I guess the only way to stop him is to lose my virginity."

Blake looked away, embarrassed, but Elsa shook her head.

"No, that's only one way, and it might not stop this Gavin person."

"You think he might still kill Maya for her Seer's blood, even if she's not a virgin?" asked Blake.

Elsa nodded.

"Great. So what else can we do?" Maya looked at her grandmother.

"There is another option. Like I said, your blood is powerful. Not only can it bring ghosts back to life, but you can control them, too."

"Control them? How?"

"The power is inside you, my love. Here," Elsa touched a cold hand to Maya's head, "and here," she said, touching Maya's heart. "But..."

Maya gave an exaggerated sigh and rolled her eyes. "I should have known there was a 'but.' There's always a 'but.'"

"But," Elsa continued, ignoring her granddaughter's sarcasm, "you must be careful. Anyone who becomes a ghost only does so because they are very strong-willed. Otherwise there would be ghosts everywhere."

Blake nodded. "I died vowing that Gavin would not get his hands on the book."

"And he likely died vowing to hold on to it at all costs," Elsa said, looking at Maya. "As strong - one might say *stubborn* - as you are, you might not be a match for this Gavin and his men."

"So, I still have to decide. What should I do?" Maya's face scrunched up as her frustration made itself evident.

Elsa patted her cheek. "Choose wisely, sweetheart. Choose wisely." She gave Maya a quick kiss on the cheek then stepped back and began to fade away.

"Grandma, no! Wait! There's more I need to ask."

"I'm sorry, I'm not strong enough to stay. But I'll be watching..."

"Dammit!" Maya shouted, as Elsa disappeared from view.

"It's not her fault," Blake said, standing next to her. "Manifesting is hard."

"Whatever." Maya stormed into the kitchen, opened the refrigerator door, and then slammed it shut without even looking inside.

"Losing your temper won't help."

"Easy for you to say." She kicked the leg of the kitchen table. "I either have to have sex or risk my life doing a Jedi knight imitation to defeat some hundred-year-old ghosts."

Blake frowned. "What is a Jedi knight?"

"Never mind." She went back to couch and practically threw herself onto the cushions. "I can't take a chance on fighting Gavin. That just leaves sex. So, how do you want to do it?"

Sitting down across from her, Blake shook his head. "It can't be me. As much as I...I've come to love you, and would welcome being human again, I couldn't stand to lose you when you grew older."

"I wouldn't leave you." But even as she said it, she knew she was lying. It was one thing to be eighteen or nineteen, or even twenty-one, and date someone who looked a little younger. They could lie about Blake's age, say he was older than he looked. But what about when she was thirty? Or forty? He would look more like her son than her lover.

And I could never have children...

"Wait," she said, as an idea came to her. "What about protection?"

"What?" Blake's face got that blank look that meant they'd hit on another generation gap in vocabulary.

"Condoms." She ignored another round of blushing, something she seemed to be doing too much of lately, and explained what they were. "No blood touching you means no becoming human again."

"No, we can't take the chance. What if all that's needed is a few drops? One accidental touch..." He left the rest unsaid.

Maya sighed. He was right. "So, what do we do?"

Hesitantly, Blake said, "There is always Stuart..."

"No freakin' way."

He shrugged. "The only other thing we can do is find the key and destroy the book before Gavin finds them and completes his ceremony."

"So, let's do that."

"It means going to the museum. And I'm not strong enough to protect you from Gavin and his men."

"Not by yourself you're not," Maya said, an idea forming in her mind. "But what if I bring friends?"

"Friends?"

"Yeah. The ones you're going to meet tomorrow night. At the dance."

"The dance? You mean, we're still going?"

"Going? I wouldn't miss it for the world. This might be my last chance to have some fun before I die. And believe me, we're gonna rock the house down."

As frightened as she was about the dangerous turn her life had taken, Maya couldn't help but burst into laughter at the look on Blake's face.

Chapter 17

The minute Maya woke up on Saturday morning she grabbed her cell and called Lucy. "Get your lazy butt out of bed. We're going shopping. I need a dress for the dance."

Maya had to hold the phone away from her ear to avoid Lucy's deafening scream. After calming her friend down, they agreed to meet at the diner in an hour.

"I can't believe you picked Blake," Lucy said, as they entered Sears, Coronado Bay's only department store. "I thought for sure your hot-and-heavy for Gavin would win that contest."

"Not anymore. I found out his bad boy look isn't just a look. He's dangerous."

"Dangerous like he drinks and drives, or dangerous like he robs liquor stores?" Lucy asked, leading the way to the dress department.

"Dangerous like he might have something to do with that girl getting murdered in the museum."

"Whoa." Lucy gave a low whistle. "That is not good."

"Yeah. Plus, it turns out he was only interested in getting into my pants, and then he was going to dump me." Maya felt bad about twisting the truth, but figured it was all right since she'd be telling Lucy everything later anyhow.

"Bastard. Stay the hell away from him."

"That might not be so easy." Maya picked a black dress with sparkling sequins from the rack, examined it, and put it back. "He's majorly whacked. Like, worse than Stuart. Grade-A stalker. I might have to do something about it."

"Call the cops." Lucy held up a short-cut, clingy red dress that looked like it would show a lot of cleavage. "Too slutty for you. But I might buy it."

"Go for it. I can't call the police. I've got no real proof, so all they can do is question him, and then he'll come after me even worse. But I have an idea for how to take care of Gavin and his asshole buddies for good. We'll tell you all about it at the dance tonight."

"Tonight? I can't wait that long. Fill me in, girl."

Maya shook her head. "Not yet. We're gonna need the whole crew, so I want to tell everyone at once. Plus, there are some details to work out. What do you think about this one?" She held up a rose-colored dress with shoulder straps.

Lucy nodded. "It's you. Go try it on."

* * *

From behind a tall case filled with earrings, Stuart Newman watched as Maya and Lucy shopped. He'd been on his way to buy some new sneakers when he'd seen them entering the store. He'd followed them in, hoping to catch Maya alone and talk with her for a few minutes. He figured she wouldn't freak out in a public place, which would give him enough time to ask her to the dance. Convincing her to go shouldn't be too hard, not as long as he kept his cool. After all, she had to still have feelings for him.

Then he'd heard them talking about the dance and had seen them picking out dresses. He hadn't caught everything they'd said, but he'd heard enough to figure out Maya was going to the dance with that asshole Blake.

Stuart clenched his fists and fought the urge to shake some sense into her. As much as he wanted to, he knew it was the wrong place for a physical confrontation. Someone was liable to get the wrong idea, think he was getting violent with her.

On the other hand, nobody's gonna care if I put a beating on that Blake fellow. And if I don't see him around town today, I know where he'll be tonight.

Stuart turned and walked away, his head filled with different scenarios - Blake and Maya dancing, Blake and Maya kissing, Blake's hands going where she'd never let Stuart's go.

All different, but all with the same ending.

Stuart's fist smashing Blake's nose into a bloody pulp.

Chapter 18

"So who is this boy that's fifteen minutes late picking up my daughter for the big dance?" Roger Blair tapped his watch, one eye narrowed, a sure sign he was annoyed.

Maya sighed and pretended she wasn't nervous.

"Roger, relax." Emily said, and then smiled at her daughter, but she was clearly perturbed, as well. They'd both taken off from work, demanding to meet the boy who was escorting Maya to the dance.

"Kind of rude, if you ask me. In my day, we came to the door. Expected to meet the parents. Now kids just park outside and honk the damn horns."

Something in her father's complaints caught Maya's attention.

Outside.

Oh. My. God.

"Um, I'll be right back. I, uh, forgot my cell phone." Maya ran upstairs before her parents could say anything.

How could I have been so stupid?

Blake wouldn't be able to knock at the door, or even show up on the porch, unless he was with her.

Maya opened her bedroom window and looked down. Sure enough, Blake was standing there, looking as nervous as she felt.

"Blake!" she called, trying to keep her voice low.

"Maya. I--"

"I know. Go to the front door. I'll meet you there, and let you in."

"Are you sure?"

"Just do it!"

Back down the stairs she ran, not pausing as she crossed the living room to the front door.

"What's going on?" Roger asked, rising from his chair.

"He's here!" Maya knew her over-the-top excitement would bring questions later, but it was the only way to get to the door without her parents wondering why there'd been no knock or ring.

Maya threw open the door and watched as Blake materialized on the porch. "Hi, Blake."

"Um, hi."

"Maya, invite him in." Her mother's voice.

"Stay close," Maya whispered. Blake nodded as they entered the living room.

"Mom, Dad, this is Blake Hennessy. He's from, um, Boston."

Blake shook hands with each of them, Maya making sure to stand within arm's length at all times. "It's a pleasure to meet you both," he said.

Roger looked him up and down with an appraising eye. "Are you going to the dance like that?"

"Dad!" Maya said, mortified at both her father's comment and her own brain fart for not remembering Blake would still be wearing the same plain tunic and pants he'd had on when The Black Lady sank. However, Blake covered well.

"No, sir. I got out of work late, and we still have to stop at my house so I can change, and so Maya can meet my family."

"Humph. All right, then."

"Okay, we have to go now."

"Wait!" Her mother picked up a camera. "I want a picture anyhow. Stand by the couch."

"Will you show up?" Maya whispered to Blake.

"As long as we hold hands."

His palm felt cold but nice in hers as they took their places. The moment the flash went off, Maya tugged Blake's arm and aimed him at the door.

"Thanks. Goodnight. Don't wait up."

"Wait just a moment. I'd like to know who's taking my daughter out. Tell us a little about yourself, Blake."

Blake turned to Maya, a deer-in-the-headlights look on his face.

"Sorry, Dad, next time. We're already late, remember? Gotta go." She kissed her parents and dragged Blake towards the door. "See you later."

"Nice meeting you." Blake waved.

"Be home right after the dance!" her father called out, as Maya shut the door. She didn't answer. Who knew what time she'd be back? This way she could say later she hadn't lied.

That's if we get back at all.

Stop it, Maya! Don't think negative. Besides, at least the first part of the night will be fun.

She smiled and tightened her grip of Blake's hand as they started walking towards the school.

"You seem very cheerful," he said.

"Just thinking about how everyone's going to react tonight."

"You mean when they see my clothes?"

She laughed. "No. I mean when I tell them you're a ghost. I can't wait to see their expressions!"

Neither of them noticed the dark-haired, swarthy figure crouched behind the bushes lining the sidewalk.

* * *

Gavin Hamlin stood by the front door of the museum, smiling out at the night. "This is better than anything I had planned."

His enthusiasm was due to the news he'd just received from Victor Fogg, one of the sailors from the Black Lady. He'd had Victor following Blake, knowing the love-sotted youth would eventually lead him to Maya. He'd hoped only to find out where she'd be, so he could overpower her and finally claim her blood for his own.

Instead, Fogg had overheard Blake and Maya talking about coming to the museum later, to - of all things - confront Gavin.

"So, what be your plan when they get here?"

Gavin turned and found Anton Childs and another sailor, Nigel Murphy, standing with Fogg. All had expectant looks on their faces. When he spoke, their smiles grew wider, but not friendly.

"My friends, tonight we bathe in blood."

* * *

Blake held Maya's hand in a painfully tight grip as they entered the gymnasium. She was about to tell him to ease up, until she realized how overwhelmed Blake, a child of a different century, must be by the scene before them.

A local band was on the stage, playing energetic, if not exactly perfect, covers of the latest pop hits. Mirror balls hung from the ceiling, tossing multicolored beams of light around the room. Tables dressed in the school colors of blue and gray had been set up throughout the gym, matching electric votive candles adding their flickering glow to the almost psychedelic setting. Several dozen couples were already dancing in front of the stage, while others milled around at tables or the buffet area.

"Don't let it get to you," Maya said, placing her lips near Blake's ear. "You'll get used to the noise in a minute."

He nodded, his disbelief evident on his face. Before he could say anything, Lucy appeared in front of them, her black leather dress garishly clashing with the pinks, blues, and reds of the other girls nearby.

"You made it!" Her cheeks were flushed and her hair slightly frazzled, leading Maya to believe her friend had either indulged in some alcohol before arriving or had just finished a heavy make out session with her date for the evening, Gary Wallace.

Actually, knowing Lucy, it was probably both.

"Told you I'd be here. We had a...slight delay."

Lucy gave Blake an unabashedly admiring glance. "I'll bet. Anything you want to share?"

"Not that kind of delay." Turning to Blake, Maya added, "Blake, this is Lucy. Don't mind her. She's got the dirtiest mind and mouth of anyone I know. Back in your day she'd have probably been a street walker."

"And loving it," Lucy said, winking at Blake. Then she frowned. "Wait a minute. Back in your day? What the hell does that mean?"

"It means we have to talk." Placing a hand on Lucy's arm, Maya steered her out to the main foyer and, then, into a short hallway housing the metal shop classrooms. Blake trailed a few steps behind, still awestruck by the size of the building.

"What's with the secrecy?" Lucy asked.

"There's something I've never told you before. But tonight I have to 'cause I need your help."

Maya's serious tone caught Lucy's attention. "So share. You know I'm here for you."

With the time finally arrived, Maya found herself at a loss for words. Where to start? How did you tell your best friend you have a supernatural power?

Maybe the best thing is to just say it. That's what Lucy would do, after all.

Taking a deep breath, Maya prepared to tell Lucy everything.

And then an all-too-familiar voice interrupted.

"Well, look who's here. Miss Virgin-a-Teen and the slut-bag."

Maya grimaced as Mary Ellen Gordon, sycophants in tow, approached them.

"Not now, Mary Ellen. We're busy."

"Busy?" Mary Ellen glanced at Blake and gave a derisive snort. "With what? Showing the homeless a good time? Let me guess. You feed him and, then, Lucy --"

"Don't go there, bitch, unless you want to spend the rest of the night in the hospital." Lucy raised a small bony fist at the gathered cheerleaders.

"Right. As if I'd ruin my makeup or a five-hundred-dollar dress before the dance even gets started." Mary Ellen motioned to the three girls standing behind her. "C'mon. I'm bored with these losers. Let's go have some real fun."

Lucy opened her mouth to say something, but Maya stopped her. "Not now, okay? Focus. Something important, remember?"

Lucy continued to glare at the departing Mary Ellen, but nodded. "Okay, shoot."

Like a suddenly-opened pressure valve, the words exited Maya in a rush.

"Ever since I was a little girl I could see ghosts and talk to them, and now there are evil ghosts in town who are trying to kill me so they can come back to life, and I need your help to get rid of them."

Maya stopped, waiting for Lucy's reaction.

For a moment, Lucy just stared at her with a blank expression. Then, she burst out laughing. When she could finally speak, she was holding her chest.

"Oh, my God! That was priceless! Did you think of that on your own, or did Blake help you? Blake, you just went to the top of my fav's list. I..." she paused, looking around the hallway.

"Hey, where'd he go?"

Maya turned and saw Blake standing ten feet down the hall, far enough away that her presence would have no effect on him, rendering him invisible to everyone but her.

She immediately understood his plan.

"It's no joke, Lucy. I'll prove it to you. Blake, come here."

"Girl, you're pure loco. There's no one...oh, holy shit!"

Although to Maya it appeared as if Blake was simply walking down the hall, she could imagine what Lucy saw. A shimmering form gradually coalescing into a transparent image, which then grew steadily more solid as it approached. By the time Blake got within five feet of Maya, he looked as solid as a living person.

Under her makeup, Lucy's face went pale; and when she turned back to Maya, her expression was unreadable.

"This isn't funny. What are you trying to pull?"

Maya took Blake's hand and held it out towards Lucy. "Touch him."

Lucy's hand trembled slightly as she reached forward and placed two fingers on Blake's palm. The moment they touched, she pulled back. "Dude, you are ice cold."

Letting go and taking two steps back, Maya said, "Now touch him again."

Lucy gasped as her hand went right through Blake's. "That's...I...ohmyfreakin' God." She swung her hand back and forth through his arm, and then his chest. "That is like totally awesomely stupendous!"

Something relaxed in Maya's chest, and she let out a breath she hadn't realized she'd been holding. "You're not mad?"

"I was for a minute, but that's 'cause I thought you were trying to pull a 'Scare Tactics' on me. This is just too cool for words. Dude, you're a ghost? A real ghost?"

Blake nodded.

"Where'd you come from? How'd you get here? Are all ghosts as hot as you?"

"Lucy, focus. I've got a problem, remember?"

"Huh? Oh, yeah. More ghosts. Bad ones. What's the deal with that?"

It took Maya several minutes to explain everything, and Lucy only made things worse by constantly interrupting with questions and passing her hands through Blake. When she finally got the whole story out, Maya said, "So, now I need you to come with us to the museum so we can find this book and key before Gavin does."

Lucy shook her head. "Unreal. Not only do you meet one sexy ghost, you manage to meet two. And one of them's an evil wizard. And, then there's me. All I end up with are second string football players who drink so much that half the time they can't even get a--"

"Too much information!" Maya waved her hands. "Will you do it?"

"Sure." Lucy shrugged. "No biggie. I'll tell Gary he's gotta help, or there'll be no seeing what's under this dress tonight. And Fiona and Curtis can come with us." Fiona O'Malley and Curtis DeVoy were another couple who were supposed to be meeting Maya and Lucy at the dance.

"But you can't tell them the parts about the ghosts," Maya said. "I don't want everyone knowing about...what I can do."

"Don't worry. We'll be back with the stuff before you know it." Lucy turned to leave, but Maya stopped her.

"Wait. What do you mean? We're coming with you."

Now it was Lucy's turn to look serious. "No way. You said these sailor guys want to slice you open and drain your blood. So why would you take the chance of going into the museum when we can do it without you? If you're not there, the ghosts can't hurt us." To emphasize her point, she waved her hands through Blake's head, causing him to flinch.

"Oh, crap. I never thought of that." Maya turned to Blake. "Would they be safe?"

"I, I don't know. Gavin can sometimes use his energy to make things happen, like dropping things from shelves or turning out the lights."

"Ooh, I'm scared." Lucy mimed her hands shaking. "I might get hit by a flying book. And no lights? Who cares. We'll bring flashlights. C'mon, this'll be cake. You guys enjoy the dance, and we'll be back in an hour or two in time to see Miss Mary Ellen Slutty Gordon get crowned stupid Dance Queen again."

"What do you think?" Maya asked Blake.

He shrugged. "It does seem sensible. You would be safe, and Gavin wouldn't have the book."

"Settled. Keep this one, Maya. He's got a good head on his shoulders, even if you can put your hand through it." Lucy did just that, a wide grin on her face.

"Knock it off, Lucy. How would you like it if you were a ghost and someone kept doing that?"

"Hell, if I were a ghost, I wouldn't be wasting time chasing wizards or going to dances. I'd be hangin' in the boys' locker room, enjoying the view."

She gave them a wink and a wave and headed down the hall, trailing sparkling glitter and perfume.

"Your friend is very loyal," Blake said.

"And too horny for her own good." At Blake's confused look, Maya laughed. "I'll explain while we dance. C'mon, if we've got two hours to enjoy ourselves, let's make the most of it."

Chapter 19

"This has got to be the craziest thing you have ever talked me into." Gary Wallace stared at the basement window they'd just jimmied open. The museum, still closed because of the murder, was dark and quiet. "Why can't Maya just call the police?"

"I told you, she's got no proof. That's why it's up to us to get her out of trouble." She hiked up her dress, knelt down, and crawled headfirst through the window. In the process, her dress rode high enough to show everyone her matching thong.

"Hey, Lucy. The moon's sure full tonight," Curtis said with a snicker, earning a punch on the arm from Gary.

"Enjoy the view, Curtis. It's as close as you're gonna get." Lucy shook her butt at them before dropping down into the basement. Just as her feet disappeared from view, the sound of breaking glass reached the three teens standing by the museum's foundation. Gary quickly knelt and peered through the window.

"Lucy, you okay?"

"Yeah, I'm cool," came her voice from the darkness. "I knocked something over. Hand me the flashlight."

Gary stuck his hand through and moved the light around until Lucy's face appeared like a floating head. She took the light and then stepped back, aiming it at the table under the window so the others could see where to land as they crawled through.

Once inside, Gary led them out of the storage room and into a hallway. Footsteps echoing in the silent building, they moved slowly through the dim light cast by the emergency exit lamps and the scattered ceiling bulbs left on by the staff.

"This is so creepy," Fiona whispered.

"It's worse than the library," said Lucy.

"Shhh," hissed Gary, holding a finger over his lips. "You want to get arrested?"

It only took a few minutes, and one wrong turn, for them to find their way to the stairs and up to the main floor. Before opening the stairwell exit, Fiona stopped them.

"What about the guards?"

"There're two of them, according to Blake," Lucy told them. She'd previously explained that Blake worked at the museum part time. "They check each room once per hour, but all they do is walk through and go on to the next exhibit. When we hear them coming, we just hide 'til they leave."

"Easier said than done," Gary said. He tugged at the collar of his white tuxedo shirt, unaware he was smearing grimy fingerprints across the material.

"I'll make it worth your while, I promise." Lucy rubbed against him and gave him a quick kiss, then left him clutching at empty air as she turned and pushed the door open a crack.

"Hallway's empty. Let's go."

Thanks to the museum's marble floors, high ceilings, and cement walls, the atmosphere was even more cave-like than the lower hallways had been, amplifying the *click-clock* of the girls' shoes until it sounded as if several horses were traversing the hall.

"Jesus, they don't need alarms in here," Gary whispered. "The guards can probably hear us from across the building."

"Let's hope not," Fiona said. "I can't run in these heels."

"You do know where we're going, don't you?" Curtis asked, as Lucy paused by a set of doors.

"Of course. Unlike some people, I actually attended class the day we came here."

Gary cleared his throat. "Only 'cause Maya made you."

"The reason doesn't matter. C'mon." She pulled open a door and peeked inside. "This is it." She motioned for the others to follow.

With the lights dimmed low and the empty museum shrouding them in an eerie silence, the Black Lady exhibit looked nothing like it had during the class trip. Anchors, trunks, and glass cases magically morphed into weirdly threatening shapes. Shadows seemed larger than they should be. Furtive movements took place at the corner of the eye, disappearing when viewed head on.

"This place is majorly freaky," Curtis said in hushed tones.

"How are we supposed to find this book and key?" Fiona asked. "We don't even know where to look."

"Behold, weenies, you have the answers in your hands." Lucy flicked her flashlight back on. "It's just a dumb old museum, you dorks. Just start searching through stuff. Fiona, stand by the door and listen for anyone coming."

Lucy, Gary, and Curtis spread out, their flashlights darting around the dark room like drunken spotlights at a concert. Fiona took a spot by the room's entrance, leaning against one of the heavy doors and alternating between watching her friends and stealing glances into the hallway.

"Isn't this the room where that girl got murdered?" Curtis asked.

"No, that was - ow!"

The others turned at Gary's startled exclamation.

"What happened?" Lucy shined her flashlight on him. He was shaking his hand like he'd burned a finger.

"Something gave me an electric shock."

Lucy bit her lip, remembering Blake's warning about Gavin. Were the psycho spirit and his pals in the room with them? Was one of them watching her, maybe right next to her? She shivered, and then told herself to stop being so silly. Without Maya, the ghosts were as impotent as an old man without his Viagra. If a tiny shock was the best they could do, they had nothing at all to worry about.

Gary had already returned to sorting through the items on a table, so Lucy went back to what she'd been doing, which was running her hands along the bottom of the old desk from the captain's quarters, hoping to locate some kind of secret drawer or compartment.

Finding nothing, she stood up and was about to open one of the drawers when an intricately carved tobacco box tumbled over onto the floor from a nearby table.

"Shit!" Lucy jumped back, wondering which ghost had done it. According to Blake, there were several roaming around. A sudden chill passed across her shoulders, and she waved her arms back and forth, trying to dislodge it.

"Lucy?" Gary aimed his light at her.

Behind him, a wooden dish slid off a table.

"Dammit!"

Across the room, Fiona made shushing noises. "For God's sake, be quiet, you guys. The guards will hear us."

A fluorescent light in one of the display cases flickered on and then went dark.

Something hit the floor with a metallic clatter.

Three flashlights swung around, searching for the source of the noise. "Jesus, what the hell's going on?" Curtis's voice cracked as he looked back and forth.

"Just ignore it and keep looking," Lucy said, doing her best to pretend her own hands weren't shaking. "The sooner we're out of here--"

Her flashlight went out.

"Knock it off, asshole!" she shouted, shaking the light.

"I didn't do anything." Gary frowned at her.

"Not you. I--" she stopped as the flashlight turned on again. "Never mind. I'm just freaked."

All three flashlights went dark.

Lucy moaned and shivered as something cold brushed against her neck.

"That's it, we're outta here." Gary grabbed her hand and headed for the doors, where Fiona was just another dark shadow among many in the cavernous room.

"Right behind you, man," Curtis said. His flashlight rattled as he tried to shake it back to life.

Fiona stepped away from the doors. "You guys are making enough noise to wake the dead. Did you at least find the stuff?"

As if in response, the ceiling lights flashed on and off. Sparks flew from metal objects on the display tables, creating glowing, whirling orbs of multi-colored light that disappeared as quickly as they'd formed, leaving purple after-images in their eyes.

A tall display cabinet near Fiona began shaking, the items inside falling off their shelves.

Lucy had a horrible premonition. "Fiona, look out!"

The blonde girl stared at the vibrating case but didn't move. "Holy crap, it's an earth--"

The glass window exploded outwards. Fiona cried out as razor-sharp fragments sliced through her flesh. Warm liquid splashed across Lucy's face, bitter and salty on her tongue and lips. She bent over and gagged, trying to get the taste out of her mouth.

"Fiona!" Curtis pushed past them, grabbed his girlfriend as she collapsed to the floor. All the lights in the room came on, blinding them with white-hot brilliance and sparkling off the dozens of crystalline spears jutting from Fiona's shredded face.

"Call 911!" Curtis knelt beside Fiona, his eyes wide, cradling her head in his lap. Splashes of blood covered his gray tuxedo.

Gary pulled out his cell phone, then shouted in frustration when he couldn't get a signal. "No service!"

"Gavin." At first Lucy wondered who'd said his name, then recognized the voice as her own. "Oh, God, no. This wasn't supposed to happen."

With a bang, the doors flew open, causing Lucy to cry out. Two security guards stood there, flashlights in hand.

"What the...?"

"We need an ambulance!" Curtis shouted.

At that moment, more blood sprayed out from Fiona's body. At first, Lucy thought she was hallucinating, as the blood didn't seem to be falling back to the ground. Then, she realized it was taking shape in the air.

A human shape.

Like a picture coming into focus, the body of a young man appeared before them, his white shirt and black long coat smeared with Fiona's blood.

He pointed at Lucy and nodded. "You must be dear Maya's friend. My thanks to you."

"Thanks for what?" Gary placed himself between Lucy and the stranger. "Who the hell are you?"

"For bringing a virgin to me."

Lucy shook her head. "No. No, it's not supposed to work like that."

The figure started to say something, but one of the security guards interrupted.

"I don't know what's going on, but I want all of you on the ground. Now!" He drew his stun gun from its holster, and his partner did the same.

The man in black whirled around, pointing his finger at the two guards. "Silence!" Bolts of bluish-white electricity exploded from the stun guns, knocking both guards to the ground. They hit the floor, their legs twitching, their hands and shirts scorched and smoking.

"What the fu - oof!" The rest of Gary's words disappeared as Gavin's fist hit his stomach, doubling him over. A second punch sent him to the floor.

"Stop it!" Lucy shouted.

Gavin laughed and pointed at Fiona's body. "Hurry, my friends, before it is too late."

"Stay the hell away from her." Curtis placed himself between Fiona and Gavin, his fists raised and ready.

He never saw the two additional bodies taking shape behind him, invisible hands appearing as they smeared the dying girl's blood over themselves. Lucy did, but it was too late. One of the new figures struck Curtis from behind.

Then, all three of them turned their attention to Lucy. Gavin stepped forward and placed a freezing cold hand, wet and sticky with blood, under her chin, forcing her to look up at him.

"Now, little girl. It's time to finish things."

Chapter 20

Mary Ellen Gordon motioned for Kelly Pasternak and Sandi Taylor to keep quiet. "This is going to be priceless," she whispered. "That little fire-crotch bitch is going to regret mouthing off to me."

They'd seen Lucy and the others exit the dance, serious looks on all their faces, leaving Maya and her scrungy, underdressed date behind. Mary Ellen's first thought was that the two crazy BFFs had been arguing, but then she'd seen Maya and her boyfriend smiling and looking all lovey-dovey as they did poor imitations of dancing.

That was when Mary Ellen knew something was up. And if it involved Little Miss Easy Pants, odds were good it was probably illegal, or potentially embarrassing, or both.

So she'd grabbed Kelly and Sandi and told them to follow her - that they were going to play a little practical joke on Lucy. They'd stayed a block behind the foursome, keeping to the shadows and constantly shushing each other whenever one of them complained about their shoes or dress getting ruined.

From across the street, they'd watched in stunned amazement as Lucy and the others broke into the museum.

This is better than I'd hoped for, Mary Ellen thought. She'd expected something typically juvenile, like spray painting a building or TP-ing some teacher's car or house.

But breaking into a public building?

Priceless!

"C'mon, let's go," she said, after giving the loser crew a few minutes. "I want to catch them in the act."

"What, inside?" Kelly's voice carried an unmistakable tone of defiance, something Mary Ellen wasn't used to. "No way. I'm not crawling through some window in this dress. Just call the cops."

"No. I'm going to deliver the proof to the police myself," Mary Ellen said, holding up her cell phone. Like everything else she owned, it was top of the line with excellent photo and video capabilities.

"Then you can go without me. I paid a lot of money for this dress. I'm not ruining it for a prank. I'm going back to the dance."

"Fine. Sandi and I will do it. Right, Sandi?"

"Um...no, I don't think so Mary Ellen. I mean, like, Kelly's right. We look hot in these dresses, you know? The last thing I wanna do is tear it, or get dirt and stuff all over it. Besides, the guys are waiting for us."

"I don't believe you two. This is the chance of a lifetime. Don't you wanna see that bitch in jail?" Mary Ellen tried one of her famous pouts, but in the near-dark it didn't have the desired effect.

"Not if it means going back to the dance looking like a thrift-store reject. You can play Sherlock Holmes if you want. I vote for dancing and having fun. C'mon, Sandi, let's go."

The two girls walked away.

"Fine. Be that way. When everyone's talking about this tomorrow, you'll wish you were with me." Neither girl answered.

Unbelievable, Mary Ellen thought, as she crossed the street. *Well, who needs them? Now I can get all the glory. When Monday comes around, Lucy's arrest will be the talk of the school and I'll be the one everyone wants to talk to. I might even get my name in the paper!*

Cell phone securely in hand, she knelt down in the damp grass and lowered herself into the darkness of the museum basement.

She'd only taken two steps when cold, wet hands grabbed her. She opened her mouth to scream, but only a weak gasp came out.

"Well, what have we here?" a rough male voice asked. He was no more than a gray shadow against the shadows. "Another mouse come to play."

"Should we bring her upstairs with the others?" a second man asked.

"Aye, but I'm thinking we should bleed her first. See if she's got virgin blood for Mister Hamlin."

Something sharp stabbed Mary Ellen in the arm, and that was when she finally found her voice.

By then, Kelly and Sandi were too far away to hear her screams.

* * *

"...The magic, the magic of love, is inside you..."

Maya smiled against Blake's chest as she hummed along to the song. It *was* magic. What else but magic could explain the transformation of a drafty gymnasium into the most romantic place on Earth? The couples dancing around them. The rainbow sparkles of the lights reflecting off the disco globes and glassware and girls' dresses. The balloons and streamers dangling in the air like crystalline rainbows.

The whole night was magic.

"I'm so glad we came tonight," she said, pitching her voice just loud enough so Blake could hear it above the music.

"I am, too. I've never experienced anything like this before."

Maya closed her eyes and let Blake guide her around the dance floor to the slow ballad, one hand in hers and the other lightly touching her waist. Her attempt to teach him some modern dance moves had failed miserably, so she'd told him to show her how they danced in his time. She didn't know what it was they were doing - a waltz? - but it reminded her of how they danced in the old black and white movies her parents liked to watch, all moving in circles and swaying back and forth.

She always worked up a good sweat from dancing, and the cool chill Blake radiated was a welcome relief as they glided around the dance floor. *Like having my own personal air conditioner.*

The song ended all too soon, and the band picked up the pace, jumping into the latest hit by last year's American Idol winner. Knowing Blake wouldn't have a chance on the dance floor, she took him by the hand and led him to the snack table.

"I thought you wanted to dance," he said.

"Maybe you don't eat or drink, but I'm thirsty." Maya downed a cup of soda and then immediately regretted it when she couldn't hold in a loud belch.

"Oh my God. I'm so sorry. I'm not usually such a gross-out."

Blake smiled. "In my time, it was nothing to be embarrassed about. You simply said 'Pardon me' and continued talking or eating. It was the same if someone farted."

"Eew. I will *not* be farting in front of...why are we talking about farts?" Maya put down her glass. "Let's go back to--" She stopped as someone tapped her on the shoulder.

"Hello, Maya."

"Stuart." She turned and faced him, her good mood evaporating.

"Maya--" Blake began, but she stopped him.

"It's okay. He won't do anything stupid in public. Will you, Stuart?"

He glowered at her, but took a careful step back. "No. I just wanted to say *you* look nice tonight." He gave Blake a sneering look, which Maya understood to be a putdown of his clothing. *If only he knew...*

"Thanks." She kept her voice cold.

"Maybe you'll have time for one dance with--"

Maya gasped. "Time! Holy crap. Nice talking to you, Stuart. We've got to go." She pulled Blake with her out to the dance floor.

"So, are we dancing again?" Blake asked, when Maya just stood there, staring at her cell phone.

"Look," she said, holding the phone out towards him. "It's after ten-thirty, and Lucy hasn't called or come back."

"Do you think something's wrong?"

She chewed her lip. "God, I hope not. If anything's happened to her..."

Blake put his arms around her. "The ghosts can't hurt them, remember? Maybe they haven't found the book yet. Or perhaps they just wanted to give us some time alone together."

Maya smiled. "Knowing Lucy, it's more likely she's having a quickie in the museum bathroom. I'll explain later," she added, seeing his confused look.

"How about this? We wait another quarter hour; if she hasn't come back, we go to the museum and look for her."

Something loosened in Maya's chest. Maybe she was just being a nervous Nellie, as her grandmother would say.

If she's off somewhere knocking boots while I'm worrying my ass off, I'll kill her.

"Okay," she said to Blake. "Fifteen minutes. Then, we go."

"Good. That gives me time to show you one more dance..."

* * *

Lucy fought to keep from throwing up as she tried to focus on the blood-splashed man standing in front of her.

Gavin. His name is Gavin.

And, he's going to kill us like he killed Fiona.

She'd regained consciousness just as two of Gavin's men brought a struggling, screaming Mary Ellen into the exhibit room.

"Caught another one, sir," one of the sailors had said. He'd pushed Mary Ellen to the floor, and Lucy had noticed she was bleeding from a cut on her arm.

"Excellent." Gavin took a knife from one of the men and lifted Mary Ellen by the throat. "Another virgin delivered for our pleasure?"

Mary Ellen had shaken her head violently. "No! No, I'm not the one you--"

Quick as a viper, Gavin's hand flashed out and back again. Mary Ellen's head fell back, exposing a wide gash. For a split second it gaped like a giant mouth, and then a red fountain of blood burst forth.

Gavin reached out and caught some of the blood as Mary Ellen's body toppled to the floor. He squeezed his fist and red squirted out between his fingers.

The sailors stared at him in silent anticipation.

"Nothing." He opened his hand and shook it, sending droplets everywhere. "She was no more a virgin than I am. Get back to work."

With Mary Ellen's grisly murder looming in her memory, Lucy expected the thought of her imminent death to send her into a panic, but it didn't. She assumed she was in shock. Either that, or the blow to the head she'd taken had hurt her worse than it felt. Not that it mattered. Gagged and bound in the middle of the exhibit room, there wasn't much she could do except wait for Gavin to turn the knife on her. Gary and Curtis were still unconscious. Fiona's body lay where she'd died, surrounded by a pool of blood. Mary Ellen's was draped over a table, her head nearly separated from her body. The two guards looked like they were dead, as well.

It's all so wrong. How did it go wrong? They weren't supposed to...

Why haven't they killed us yet?

Wearing expressions of sullen disappointment, the two sailors had joined their companions in turning over tables, tearing exhibits apart, and smashing chairs. But not Gavin. He walked back and forth in front of his prisoners, staring at them.

As if he were waiting for something.

But what?

One of the sailors cursed. "Dirty bastard!"

Gavin turned quickly at the man's shout, but he didn't appear surprised.

"What is it, Anton?"

"Me hand. Went right through the table. It's like--"

Lucy jumped as the man disappeared in mid-word. She looked at another sailor just in time to see him fade into nothingness, his eyes wide as an owl's.

Gavin swung around and faced Lucy, his body already turning transparent. "Be damned! An ordinary virgin still isn't enough. We need the witch's blood if we're to become human again. Rest assured, I'll make sure she comes to us. Her life for yours. Pray that she--"

He was gone.

Dammit! Lucy struggled to free her hands, but the ropes were too tight. *Of course, they are. Who ties better knots than freakin' sailors?*

She continued twisting and turning anyhow, hoping to loosen the bindings, or find something sharp on the floor. Although her dress kept tangling around her legs, she managed to roll over and kick at Gary and Curtis, but neither of them woke up.

There's got to be something I can do before they bring Maya here.

The guards. They had to have something on them she could use. Guns. Knives.

Radios.

That's it! I can call for help.

Now all she had to do was roll and caterpillar crawl across a huge room filled with tables and other obstacles, all before the ghosts brought her best friend back. Praying Gavin didn't decide to drop a cabinet on her, she put her plan in motion.

Her first attempt ended with her legs smacking painfully against a broken chair. Cursing and crying into the foul-tasting gag, she maneuvered her body around to a different angle.

I'll be damned if some stupid ghosts are going to kill me. Or any more of my friends.

Even as she started rolling again, she had a sinking feeling her tough words weren't going to be good enough.

* * *

"What time is it?" Blake asked, as he guided Maya off the dance floor.

"It's been twenty minutes. I can't take it anymore. We're going. It's not like Lucy to--" She paused as Blake's eyes went wide. "What's wrong?"

"Trouble." He pointed towards the entrance to the gym.

Two of Gavin's men stood just inside the doors. One was heavily bearded, the other clean-shaven with a scarred face, and both wore furious expressions. Because they were so far away from Maya, they were translucent images, barely there at all. She knew no one else would even be able to see them, as long as they came no closer to her.

One of the sailors pointed at them and motioned towards the doors. Maya felt a chill run through her as she recognized their faces.

"Those are the men who attacked me on the sidewalk."

Blake gripped her hand. "Gavin must have sent them. This cannot be a good thing."

The two men entered the room, gradually gaining solidity as they drew closer to Maya. Although the party lighting kept people from noticing the transformation, the two figures drew more than a few stares because of their age and clothing. By the time they stopped in front of Maya and Blake, all eyes were on them.

"We have a message, witch," one of them said, pointing a callused finger at Maya. "If you want your friends to live, come with us."

"We are not going--"

Maya cut off Blake's retort. "We'll come."

Blake turned to her. "It could be a trick. Lucy might be perfectly safe, even returning as we speak."

"She's my best friend. I can't take that chance." She didn't know how to explain it any better than that. Either he'd understand or he wouldn't. But she wasn't going to let anything happen to Lucy. Especially when it was her fault her friends were in trouble.

I should have never let them go. If anything happens to her, to them...

The sailors turned and headed for the door. Maya followed close behind them, dragging Blake along with her, so no one would catch a glimpse of the ghosts fading out. Several of her classmates put their hands out or asked questions, but she kept walking, ignoring their attempts to stop her.

When they reached the sidewalk, she let go of Blake's hand. "You don't have to come. But I'm going."

"I'm not leaving your side."

When he placed his hand back in hers, she thought her knees might give out on her. She'd expected him to continuing arguing, or maybe even just disappear, let her go on her own.

How ironic. Of all the guys in Coronado Bay, the only one who's truly faithful and dependable isn't even alive.

As much as she wanted to throw her arms around him and kiss him, there was no time. The two sailors were already walking away.

I'm coming, Lucy. Hang in there.

* * *

Stuart Newman stood on the steps of the school and watched Maya and her new boyfriend hurry down the sidewalk towards the center of town. For a moment, he lost sight of the two rough-looking men, but then they were back, right in front of Maya.

Must have been shadows.

He'd noticed the men when they'd confronted Maya and her new boyfriend at the prom - who hadn't? - and seen the horrified look on Maya's face when they spoke to her. He couldn't hear what they said, but it had to be real bad.

Not that I should care. Serves her right if she's in trouble. She wants to dump me for some loser? I can get a dozen girls better than her.

None of these thoughts stopped him from descending the steps and following them.

Chapter 21

Once they were inside the museum, it didn't take long for Maya to realize things were worse - far worse - than she'd imagined. Bloody handprints and footprints marred the normally spotless hallways, but that was nothing compared to the shambles of the Black Lady Exhibit. When the sailors opened the doors, Maya stopped at the sight of all the destruction. Tables and cases overturned, furniture broken, pieces of the ship and its contents scattered all over the floor.

And blood everywhere.

As soon as he saw them, Gavin signaled to his men, who grabbed her and Blake and roughly guided them to where Gary and Curtis lay tied and gagged. Along the way, they found Lucy wedged between a table and a fallen curio case, her hands and ankles cut from trying to use a piece of broken glass to slice through her bonds. She'd managed to pull her gag off, and it dangled from her neck.

"Lucy!" Maya tried to go to her, but the sailor holding her tightened his grip, each finger pressing so hard she knew she'd have bruises for a week.

If I live to see them.

"Bring the other one back, as well," Gavin said, nodding towards Lucy, who kicked and screamed to no avail as another sailor hoisted her up and led her forward. Only then did Gavin address Lucy directly.

"It was quite amusing watching you try and escape. Pity you weren't better at it. But the time for games is past." He turned to Maya. "If you give yourself to me right now, no one else has to get hurt."

"No one--?" Maya looked at Lucy, who had tears in her eyes.

"Fiona. They...they killed her. Used her blood, but they didn't stay solid. They killed Mary Ellen, too, but her blood didn't do anything."

"Oh, God." Maya felt like the earth had opened up and swallowed her. Fiona and Mary Ellen dead, and it was all her fault. "I..."

"You don't have time to waste," Gavin said. "Your choice is simple. Either you give yourself to me and your friends live, or I take what I want and they all die."

The sailor holding Lucy yanked on her hair, drawing a scream.

"All right!" Maya's thoughts were a confused blur. "But how do I know you won't kill them anyway?"

Gavin gave a nasty laugh, and she wondered how she'd ever found him the least bit attractive. "You don't, witch. But at least you'll die knowing you did all you could to save them."

"Maya, don't do it. He won't keep his word." Blake implored her as much with his eyes as with his voice.

What to do? She wanted to shout for help, cry for her mother or father. This wasn't the kind of decision a sixteen-year-old girl should have to make. Raped and killed to maybe save her friends? If she said yes, then Gavin and his men would be part of the real world forever, able to carry out his evil plans and basically turn the world into a living hell.

Say no, and the same thing happened.

That's not how choices are supposed to work!

She looked over at Lucy again, who was staring at the floor and crying. Glanced at Blake, who shook his head "no."

She knew there was only one thing to do.

"All right." She stared directly at Gavin, whose smile grew even wider, and, if possible, more malicious. "You win. I'm yours."

Gavin stepped forward and reached for her. The two men holding Maya let go. Remembering her sensei's instructions, she let Gavin draw her close.

Then, she brought her knee up between his legs as hard as she could.

"Aaaa!" He doubled over, holding both hands to his injured groin. As he did so, Maya took a step back and brought her knee up again, this time right into Gavin's face. The *snap* of his nose breaking sounded loud as a gunshot in the quiet of the museum.

Knowing it was her only chance to save her friends, Maya spun on her heel and lashed out with her other foot, catching the kneecap of the man holding Lucy. He cried out and fell to the floor, clutching his leg.

"Get out of here!" Maya shouted. "They can't hurt you if you're not near me!"

Bright lights exploded behind her, and she turned to see Blake pulling away from the two men who'd been holding him. He pointed at Maya and sparks flew from his finger.

"Maya, behind you!"

Without bothering to see who was coming at her, Maya threw herself to the side just as a bolt of lightning shot out from Blake's hand. Gavin, black fluids flowing from his newly-crooked nose, gave a high-pitched yelp as the energy caught him right in the chest. He didn't go down, though. Instead, he brought his hands up and countered Blake's attack with one of his own. Blue energy zig-zagged across the space between them, so close to Maya it made her hair stand on end. Blake cried out as his body flew backwards, crashing through a wooden case and only coming to a gradual halt when he left Maya's zone of influence and lost his solidity.

That didn't stop Gavin. The taller man strode forward, his black coat whipped by an invisible wind, his eyes wide and furious. He clapped his hands together; a purple fireball took form and then shot towards Blake, who rolled to one side just before the pulsing globe landed. The remains of the display case exploded, sending glass and wood splinters through the air.

Blake got to his feet. "Maya, run! I'll hold them off." Not waiting for an answer, he ran forward and threw a right uppercut that caught Gavin under the chin. A miniature fireworks display went off where supernatural flesh met its own kind. Gavin staggered back a step, spat something dark that wasn't blood, and smiled.

"So, the mouse has grown into a man, eh? Let's see what you've got, boy."

Colored light detonated over and over again as the two men, one tall and one short, one dark and one fair, exchanged punches. Each gave as good as he got, landing and taking blows to the face and body. Maya used the opportunity to untie Lucy's ropes. For a few seconds, she actually believed she'd have a chance to get herself and her friends out of trouble, at least temporarily.

Then Gavin struck Blake a hard blow to the side of the head that sent the smaller man reeling. Before he could recover his balance, Gavin hit him twice more, once in the throat and once in the mouth.

Blake's eyes closed, and he fell to the floor.

Gavin turned to Maya, who was busy dragging Curtis towards the door, while Lucy did the same with Gary. The ghost-wizard's cruel smile would have made a shark proud.

"Now, it's time for me to take what's mine."

Chapter 22

Hiding behind one of the few display cases still standing, Stuart Newman clamped his hands over his mouth to keep from calling out. He did *not* want to draw the attention of the...the *things* fighting in the center of the room, or the ones watching, who he guessed were just as dangerous.

He thought of them as things because it was impossible to imagine them as people, even though they looked human enough - at least when he could see them. They appeared and disappeared, fading in and out of sight like--

Like ghosts?

It seemed too crazy. He'd never believed in ghosts. But it would explain a helluva lot. The disappearing acts, the lightning, the weird clothes. Ghosts from a long time ago.

From the Black Lady?

Why not? It makes as much sense as anything else.

And Maya's new boyfriend, Blake, was right in the middle of things, fighting with that other guy while Maya crouched on the floor between them. *Gavin, that's the other guy's name. I recognize him, too. He throws a mean punch for a ghost. What the hell's Maya doing with these guys?*

Whatever was going on, it looked like Blake was getting the worse of it.

Serves him right. Maya, too. If she'd stayed with me, none of this would be happening.

Mixed emotions fought their own battle inside Stuart's head and heart, mimicking the one in the middle of the room. On the one hand, he felt tempted to just sneak out the way he'd snuck in, get out of the room, and, then, simply run like hell and let Maya and Blake and Lucy and the others get what was coming to them.

On the other hand, he knew he should probably do something to help because no matter how bitchy she'd been to him, he couldn't - or at least shouldn't - let the ghosts hurt her or any other people.

That they had something very bad in mind was obvious. He'd figured that out the moment he'd seen the two security guards lying inside the exhibit room. He'd have left right then, but he'd been afraid someone might notice the exhibit room doors opening. And then he'd end up a prisoner, too.

Or worse, like the guards.

So he'd hidden, unable to tear his eyes away from the light show the two ghosts were putting on.

Then Blake went down, and things changed very quickly.

For the worse.

* * *

Maya stared at Gavin and finally understood that he was crazy. Not killing-small-animals crazy or even shooting-up-the-post-office crazy, but totally Osama Bin Laden kill-everyone-in-the-world super-villain wacko insane.

And she was the only one who could stop him.

He would kill them all if he had a chance, then the whole town, and who knew how many towns after that. She couldn't let that happen even if it meant risking death.

Or worse.

"Wait," she said, holding out her arm. "It's not the sex you need, it's just my blood. You don't even have to kill me. A few drops will do it."

Gavin shook his head. "I can't take that chance. Blood alone might not be a permanent solution to my situation."

Two more steps brought him so close she could feel the chill emanating from him. He reached out and stroked a hand through her hair, let it slide down her neck to her chest, where it cupped one breast. He squeezed just hard enough to be uncomfortable but not painful.

The look in his eyes said the pain would come soon enough.

"Besides, my way will be much more enjoyable. At least for me and my men."

Rough laughter and a couple of rude comments came from the men behind her, but Maya ignored them. It was Gavin she had to convince. She couldn't afford to focus on anything except him.

Fighting the urge to pull away from his groping fingers, she said, "What happens if you kill me, and it doesn't work?"

His fingers stopped moving. "What?"

"You killed Fiona, but you stayed a ghost. What if the same thing happens again?"

His black eyes narrowed. "It won't. 'Tis your blood that makes the difference. Your friend wasn't a witch."

Maya heard the slightest hint of uncertainty in his voice and tried not to show her growing excitement. "How do you know? Maybe it would've worked if you hadn't killed her. Do the tales say you have to sacrifice a virgin or just take the blood of a virgin?"

Gavin stepped back and his gaze moved up and past her. "Childs? What say you to that?"

A man spoke behind her. Maya recognized the voice as belonging to one of the men who'd attacked her earlier in the week, the older of the two.

"There be nothing specific about killing, in actuality. The way I always heard it was 'it takes the virgin witch's blood to bring back what's been lost.'"

Tiny sparks crackled in the air around Gavin's head and his mouth grew tight. When he finally spoke, his words carried the same chill as his body. "So, in fact, you don't know a damned thing about what to do?"

He didn't let the other man answer, just kept talking. "You can't even tell me if I'm supposed to take her virginity, her blood, her life, or some damned combination of the three?"

When the sailor called Childs answered, Maya heard more than a little fear in his voice. "Aye, sir. That be the problem with magik and spells. Too often they be murky as a foggy sea."

Gavin's voice didn't change, but when he next spoke, an involuntary shiver ran through Maya.

"Don't lecture me on spells, Mister Childs. I've plenty of knowledge in that area." The other man wisely stayed silent.

Though her body still trembled, Maya kept her voice steady as she continued her cajoling. "Gavin, listen to me. You have nothing to lose doing it my way. I'll still be your prisoner. And a virgin. If my blood doesn't work, then you can...you know. But if you try it your way first, and it fails, then what? I'm dead and useless."

Gavin stared at her for a long moment. She imagined his dark gaze digging through her brain, trying to find any trace of trickery. Finally, he nodded. "'T'would be faster, I'll give you that. And, if it doesn't work, rest assured you'll be begging for a quick death."

Before Maya could respond, he grabbed her arm in a grip that was strong as steel. Using a shard of glass from a nearby table, he dug the point deep into the meaty part of her hand below the thumb, opening a two-inch gash. Although she tried her best, Maya couldn't help but give voice to her pain as fire blossomed in her palm.

Ignoring her shout, Gavin clamped his hand over hers. The effects of the blood on him were immediate. He gasped and stepped back, his eyes wide and his mouth open in surprise.

"I feel it!" As he spoke, a white glow surrounded him, so bright it forced Maya to squint her eyes and tilt her head away. Through her tears she saw Lucy kneeling on the floor, covering her face with her arms.

In the time it took Maya to inhale and exhale, the glow faded and Gavin let out a bellow of laughter.

"It worked! I'm whole again!" He slapped his hands against his chest, sending multi-colored sparks in all directions. Thunder rumbled outside the museum, so loud and close the floor vibrated under Maya's feet.

"Hurry." Gavin motioned to his men and all five of them ran forward, pushing and shoving at each other in their haste to reach Maya. The room turned spotlight bright as one after another touched her blood and changed. One of them drew a knife and Maya cried out.

"No! Gavin, there's plenty of blood here for all of them. You still don't know if the magik is permanent."

Gavin snapped his fingers and tiny balls lightning crackled and spat against the ceiling. "She's right. We might need her yet again. And if we don't, she'll be more fun alive than dead."

The sailors burst into laughter. One of them grabbed her, his hands running up and down her body, leaving bloody streaks on the front of her dress. Another yanked her hair, forcing her head back so he could mash his lips against hers. She tried turning away, but another bearded, filthy face waited on that side, as well. Hands pawed at her from all directions.

"Enough!" said Gavin. "Plenty of time for that later. First, find the book. Then, you can play all you want."

A few of the sailors grumbled, and one muttered, "Aye, Mister Hamlin," but they all let go of her and spread out across the room, angrily scattering objects off tables and tossing things to the floor.

God, that was too close. Her plan - which wasn't much of a plan to being with - centered on staying alive a little longer. *Hopefully a lot longer. As in seventy years or so.*

She looked around, saw that none of the men were guarding her anymore. Her first thought was the doors, but she quickly saw she'd never get past the sailors on that side of the room. Instead, she knelt down next to Lucy and gave her friend a hard shake.

"Lucy! C'mon, snap out of it. I need your help."

It took a few more shakes, but eventually Lucy lifted her head, exposing tracks of black mascara running down her cheeks like bad Halloween makeup. "We're all gonna die, aren't we?"

"Hopefully, no." Maya pointed at Curtis and Gary, who still lay unconscious on the floor. "Go see if you can wake them up. Now's our only chance, while they're all busy."

"You have a plan?"

"Maybe. Just hurry."

To her credit, Lucy didn't ask any more questions, just crawled across the broken glass and wood to where the boys lay. Maya was glad for that. Saying she had a plan - even a "maybe" plan - was stretching things to the limit. "Desperate fantasy" might be more appropriate.

Still, it was their best hope.

It all went back to something Grandma Elsa had said.

"Your blood is powerful. Not only can it bring ghosts back to life, but you can control them, too."

And she'd said something else, as well. The power is inside me. My heart and my head.

The memory of that conversation had returned when Gavin touched his hand against her blood. He hadn't been the only one who'd felt the power. For a brief moment, every inch of her body, every individual cell it seemed, tingled and itched like there'd been electricity running through her. She'd felt it again each time one of the other ghosts touched her.

Can I really do it?

That was where the "maybe" came in. Not alone, that's for sure. She'd need help. So, while Lucy attempted to wake Gary and Curtis, Maya went to Blake, making sure she only touched him with the hand that wasn't bleeding.

If her plan worked, she didn't want it affecting him, as well.

"Blake. Blake, wake up. C'mon, you're a freakin' ghost, you shouldn't even be unconscious." She kept her voice to a whisper while keeping her eyes on the room to watch Gavin and his men. All had their attention focused on what they were doing, which seemed to be randomly breaking things and knocking things over.

After a minute or so - which seemed like hours to Maya - Blake moaned and opened his eyes. "Maya? Are you all right? You didn't...?"

She patted his arm. "I'm fine, and whether I did or didn't depends on what you mean. I didn't get gang raped or killed, which I consider a good thing. But I did let them have some blood. The jury's still out on whether that was a good or bad idea." She held out her hand and showed him the cut, which still oozed blood.

His hazel eyes went wide. "Oh, Maya. You mean they're...?"

"Solid, yeah." She nodded. "I had to do it, to keep us all alive. I have a plan. Or, at least I think I do. Remember what my Grandma Elsa said?"

Blake stared at her, his face blank.

"The power is in me. She said that, remember?"

He frowned. Maya wanted to shake him again, much harder this time.

"She said I can control ghosts with my blood."

Blake's eyes narrowed and the confused look disappeared. "Yes, she did say that." His growing excitement changed to concern. "She also said it was dangerous. For you."

"News flash. Look around. How much more dangerous can things get?"

As if to answer her question, Gavin gave a triumphant shout from across the room.

"I have it!" He raised his hand, and the men cheered. In the dim glow of the few remaining lights, Maya couldn't see what he held, but a nasty feeling in her stomach told her it had to be the key. Gavin confirmed her assumption a moment later when one of the sailors - the old man he'd called Childs - brought over a small trunk, and Gavin opened it.

"The book!"

Chapter 23

At Gavin's exultant cry, the sailors all stopped what they were doing and rushed across the room, laughing and shouting, ignoring Maya and the others in their haste.

"There's not much time," Childs said, as Gavin removed the book from its resting place. "'Tis near midnight. I can feel it in me bones. Aye, and 'tis, indeed, wondrous to say that again."

"That's my cue," Maya whispered to Blake. "I'm going to stall him until you and Lucy and the others are back on your feet."

"What should we do?"

Maya shook her head. "Honestly, I don't know. Just be ready to help. Or to run like hell."

She stood up and called out Gavin's name. "You have the book. Now, let us go."

Everyone turned and stared at her. Gavin pointed. "Bring her to me. She will be the first sacrifice after I open the gates. Then, her friends can follow."

"Wait!" Maya held up her hands. "You've got your book of spells or whatever, and you've got me. Why do you still need them?"

"Maya? What the hell are you doing?" Lucy's voice.

Without looking at her friend, Maya answered in a soft voice. "Take the boys and get out of here as soon as you have a chance. Get the police."

Two of Gavin's men reached her and took her by the arms. She let them drag her closer to Gavin. She still had no idea how to use the power that was supposedly inside her, but she figured the closer to her target, the better.

"'Tis true I no longer need you to regain my flesh," Gavin said. In one hand he held a dictionary-sized book, its black leather cover cracked and peeling. "But that was only necessary so I could perform the real ceremony. And, for that I need blood, as well. A lot of it. And," he added, looking at the students behind Maya, "it doesn't have to be a virgin's blood."

Turning to his men, Gavin said, "Hold them while I perform the rites."

"What rites?" It was hard not going to her friends' aid as she heard them captured once more, but the important thing was that Blake remained free.

Gavin didn't look up from the book, his fingers carefully turning each brittle, stained page. "The ones I must perform in order to call forth the *Daimones Proseoous*."

"The dammy-prosoo-whats?" A quick peek back showed Blake getting to his feet. He looked pale and weak, but his face was hard and determined. Neither of the two sailors standing near him took any notice, which was as she'd hoped. Once they'd regained their human forms, they'd lost the ability to see other ghosts. She hoped he'd figure it out, as well, and stay far enough away from her to remain invisible.

"Ancient sea daemons, known well to the Greeks. With them under my command, I'll control the oceans and have access to unlimited wealth."

Maya laughed out loud. She couldn't help it. One of the sailors gripped her arm tighter, but she ignored it. "Control the oceans? Dude, I hate to tell you this, but things have changed a little bit over the last couple of centuries. We have these things called airplanes now. They carry stuff from one country to the next through the sky. Controlling the seas would hurt the economy, but only until they like, sent some warships or subs to nuke your demon thingies back to wherever they came from."

A flicker of uncertainty passed across Gavin's face, and then his arrogant confidence returned. "If what you say is true, it is no matter. There are many other daemons, creatures of the sky, earth, and fire, and this book gives me power over them all. You'll not sway me with your words."

His fingers stopped moving, and he held the book higher. Without any pause, he started reciting words from the book. Maya cringed inside. She'd hoped he'd be like the bad guys in the movies or on TV, who took their time bragging about their plans, thus allowing the good guys to fight back.

Except now there wasn't any time. The funky book of spells was already glowing a weird greenish-yellow, which grew stronger as Gavin continued speaking.

"Hear me, foul Lords of the Deep!
In the name of Triton and Poseidon, I call you!
See the death and blackness in my heart and rejoice!

For I call to you now to give you place on Earth again!"

Enthralled by their master's words, the sailors holding Maya allowed their grips to loosen. It was the moment she'd been waiting for, the time to test her powers. Closing her eyes, she concentrated as hard as she could on the hands holding her.

Let me go. Let me go. Let me go. Let me...

The rough fingers fell away. She opened her eyes, unable to believe it had worked, afraid she'd see it was just a trick.

The two men stood like statues, eyes facing forward, arms hanging limply at their sides.

OhmyGod! It did work!

She risked a glance at Blake. He'd made it to his knees and his eyes looked more alert. He nodded to her, and she hoped he was up to his part of the plan. Then, she almost forgot what she had to do when she looked back at Gavin.

A large, ink-black oval shape was growing behind him, a floating hole in the world outlined in a sickly yellow color.

His spell! It's already taking effect.

That meant there wasn't much time. Focusing all her attention on Gavin, she repeated one command over and over, putting every ounce of strength she had left into her effort.

Look away. Look away. Look away. Look--

Gavin turned his head to the left, but didn't stop speaking.

It's now or never. C'mon, Blake!

Next to her, Blake saw the movement and extended his hands outward. The tiny hairs on Maya's arms jumped to attention as the air crackled with static electricity. Blake grunted as he loosed twin bolts of lightning from his hands right into Gavin's chest.

Where they disappeared.

Without pausing, Gavin pointed at Blake and a ruby-red line of energy lashed out. It roped itself around Blake before the stunned ghost could react, and lifted him into the air like a crazed boa constrictor choking a rat. Then, it snapped forward in whip-like fashion and sent Blake flying through the air, his body burnt and smoking even as it faded into semi-transparency. He hit the ground and didn't move.

Gavin's eyes mocked Maya with cruel amusement as he continued the spell. A stiff breeze sprang up out of nowhere and quickly turned into a heavy wind that tossed papers and small objects around the room. Maya found herself squinting against the dust and debris hitting her face.

Then she forgot all about her own discomfort as the glowing oval shape grew. Smaller than a car tire at first, it rapidly expanded until it was taller than Gavin and easily four feet wide.

Oh, God. It's growing stronger.

Seeing their last chance at defeating Gavin, Maya cursed out loud. What else could she try? Her plan had failed. She wasn't strong enough to defeat Gavin alone, and...

Wait. What if I had help? If ghosts can channel energy and turn it into lightning, maybe they can transfer some of that energy to me. It was worth a try, but how? Blake was out cold again, and even if she woke him, she doubted he had any strength left to share.

Grandma Elsa!

Not caring if Gavin heard her, she called out for her grandmother. "Grandma Elsa! Please, if you can hear me, I need your help!"

The ground rumbled beneath her feet, and she grabbed a table to keep from falling down. The few artifacts left on the remaining shelves joined their companions on the floor.

Not the response I was hoping for, Maya thought, recognizing the tremors as an effect of Gavin's continuing spell - strange, shadowy forms, indistinct, but somehow unpleasant to the eye, were taking shape inside the black circle.

Please, Grandma, there's not much time...

"Not much time for what - good heavens, what is that?"

Maya let out a startled squeal at the sound of her grandmother's voice behind her.

"Grandma! Thank God! There's no time to explain. I need your strength. Can you pass it on to me the way Blake and the others can make lightning?"

Without batting an eye, Elsa Crompton took Maya's hand in hers. "I think maybe it's possible. But there has to be physical contact."

"We're only gonna have one shot." Gripping her dead grandmother's ice-cold fingers, Maya turned her attention to Gavin. No time for tricks or subtlety.

"Drop the book. Your time is done. Drop the book, your time is done..."

Next to her, Elsa repeated Maya's words.

Gavin looked up, his eyes widening. The wind died down slightly. Behind him, the terrifying opening in space wavered around the edges. Then his brow furrowed in anger and he returned to the spell. The wind ratcheted up to storm force again, and the beastly faces in the oval seemed just a bit clearer.

He felt that!

Maya raised her voice even louder.

"Drop the book, your time is done..."

Chapter 24

Stuart's stomach churned as he watched Blake get blown away by the freaky-colored lightning. Could ghosts die? He didn't think so, but he also couldn't imagine taking that kind of punishment and not be majorly hurt.

The sight of Maya's ghost friend taking on solid form and going to her rescue - again! - had unnerved Stuart in a way the whole deadly situation hadn't managed to do. While Maya and Lucy and the other humans were trapped inside the room, there was no reason for Blake to stick around. He could've just disappeared, let that Gavin fellow - who apparently wasn't a ghost any longer - do whatever he had in mind. Left Maya to her own fate. After all, Blake wasn't in danger unless he put himself there.

The damn fool had even passed up the chance to become human again when the other ghosts touched Maya's blood. How that worked Stuart had no idea, but finding out his ex-girlfriend could bring ghosts back to life was no weirder than finding out she could talk to them.

Or that they even existed.

So what was Blake's deal? Why was he risking eternal life on the one hand and refusing the offer of a real life on the other?

Somehow, it all came down to Maya.

And that's why Stuart's stomach felt like he'd taken on the whole defensive line in a punching contest.

He's doing it for her. Thinking only of her.

Totally unselfish.

And in realizing that, Stuart had suddenly seen himself as Maya must have seen him. Selfish. Angry. Jealous.

In other words, a total douche.

I can still change, though. I can do something to help, too. And he'd tried. Only he'd had no success.

The doors to the hall refused to budge. He knew that because he'd crawled to them, fighting the heavy winds and flying debris, as soon as he'd seen that freaky thing forming behind Gavin. He'd played enough online video games, watched enough horror movies, to know a portal when he saw one. And although he had no clue where this one led, they almost always ended up with demons coming out of them, which was never a good thing.

Of course, with running for help no longer an option, he had no idea of what to do next. Attacking Gavin head on was out of the question. Maybe ghosts like Blake couldn't be killed, but dumb jocks wouldn't stand a chance against supernatural lightning.

So instead he'd remained hidden behind a wrecked cabinet, desperate to think of something he could do. Anything.

And that's when Maya had called out for her Grandma Elsa.

What the hell? Maya's grandmother died before Maya was even in kindergarten. Everyone knows th--

An old woman appeared behind Maya, a woman whose face Stuart recognized from the photos in Maya's house. She took Maya's hand, and together they started speaking.

At that moment, Stuart knew what he had to do.

* * *

"Drop your book, your time is done."

The moment Grandma Elsa joined in, Maya felt new life flowing through her. Not much, just a trickle, but it gave her hope. She took the energy and channeled it into her words, mentally throwing them at Gavin as if they were solid objects.

Her combined psychic and verbal assault had an effect. She saw it in the way Gavin ground his jaw as he spoke, the way the vein in his temple bulged out, the way he raised his voice as he repeated the words of the spell.

"Oh most hideous and cruel of species
Dwellers in the abyss and darkness
Hear my call and answer me!"

C'mon. Die, you bastard! Die!

He wasn't dying, though. In fact, he seemed to be getting stronger, gaining ground on her, as he recited the blasphemous words. The shapes behind him grew more distinct, forming into something resembling a giant face seen through a foggy, warped mirror.

The same way I'm drawing power from Grandma, he's drawing it from that damn book. Or maybe the portal itself. It's hopeless. I'll never beat him.

As if he heard her thoughts, Gavin flicked his gaze towards her and let the corners of his mouth curl up in a look that was more sneer than smile.

And, then, something happened. Someone took her other hand, the one not gripping Grandma Elsa's. For a brief moment she thought Blake had woken up and come to help. Except the hand was...warm? She turned her head, and her words caught in her throat, so great was her surprise.

"Stuart?"

"Don't stop," he said. "Let me help."

"But..."

He shook his head. "No buts. I've been a major jerk. I'm sorry."

Maya wanted to press the issue, but there was no time. "Thank you."

She opened herself to Stuart's energy and it rushed in, hot and vibrant instead of cool and gentle like Elsa's. Not much stronger, though. Not enough to shift the balance of power.

But if she could tap Stuart's energy...

She pulled her hand away, ignoring his protests. "Hurry! Get Lucy! We need her too!"

She expected him to argue like he always did. He surprised her again, though, by nodding and rushing off. Moments later, he was back, a shaken but determined Lucy holding his hand, both of them fighting their way against the fierce gale still blowing through the room.

He clasped fingers with Maya again, and this time the difference was immediately noticeable. It was like putting a finger against a live wire, except without the pain.

Across from them, Gavin's spell casting faltered. He paused and took a deep breath. When he spoke again, his voice carried a hint of pain that made Maya's heart sing.

"You're strong, but not strong enough. My will is greater, fueled years of agonizing lessons in the dark arts and nurtured by a century of waiting. In but a few moments the Great Dark Ones will enter this world, and I will see you all dead."

He returned to his spell, but Maya noticed sweat beading on his brow for the first time. No denying it. They'd hurt him.

And, if they could do it once...

"C'mon, everyone. Concentrate! We have to stop him."

Grandma Elsa moaned softly, but didn't falter. Maya felt it more than heard it. She never even had a chance to worry, as a vibrant humming filled her ears, the same sound you might hear when standing under heavy power lines. The mix of hot and cold energies flowing set her entire body buzzing, like the time she and Lucy had snuck cigarettes and a small bottle of tequila in the backyard.

She hoped she didn't end up puking like she had that night.

Gavin's body jerked, and he took a step back. His jaw clenched tighter than ever, but the anger was gone, replaced by determination and something Maya hoped was a touch of fear. He'd stopped reading from the book, and for an instant she thought maybe they'd succeeded in ending the spell. Then, she felt something hard and nasty slam against her brain, and she realized Gavin had turned all his energies towards stopping her.

Instinctively, she knew if he managed to break through her defenses, get inside her mind, she was as a good as dead. She pictured a steel dome closing around her brain, blocking the dark, slimy creature outside from getting in.

It's a test of wills. Him versus me. I have to be stronger.

Time seemed to slow down around her. Each heartbeat was a booming kettle drum inside her chest, steady and hard. *Thump! Thump! Thump!* Her peripheral vision faded away, and she saw Gavin as if through a telescope, bright and clear, outlined by the hellish glow of the gateway coming to life behind him. To her left and right, her family and friends grew blurred and indistinct. She felt each of them, though, sensed the similarities and differences of their energies as they mixed with her own.

Elsa, wise and secure and made of nothing but love.

Stuart, all traces of jealousy and anger gone now, his negativity stripped away until nothing remained but the same bullish determination that made him such a force on the football field.

Lucy, her fierce loyalty so different from the sarcastic, carefree attitude she projected to the outside world.

And still it wasn't enough. The pressure continued to build against Maya's psyche, growing more painful with each second. Foul tendrils of energy spread around her mental dome, black creepers that pushed and probed, searching for any weak points. Gavin's psychic being no longer contained any traces of pain or doubt. Instead, he radiated a feeling of confidence that he'd eventually best her.

Behind him, the grotesque beings waiting beyond the gate took on more detail. Their faces parodied human features, with twisted noses, narrow heads, and eyes that sat far to the sides, in fish-like fashion. Some had twisted horns, while others sprouted eely tentacles from their heads.

Maya forced herself to look away and concentrate harder. She, then, remembered something from her karate lessons. *It's all about focus. Focus on success, focus on the target. Do not let thoughts of failure enter the mind.*

Pretend he's a block of wood to kick.

The air around Gavin crackled with sparks and miniature flashes of lightning. Maya ignored the supernatural pyrotechnics and pictured her mental energy as a foot, lashing out and crashing through the barrier surrounding Gavin's essence.

Gavin groaned out loud, but instead of faltering, he launched an even stronger counter attack, one that hit her so hard she actually felt a sharp pain in her chest. A surprised cry escaped her, and the hands holding hers tightened in response. Her lungs froze, refusing to work, and terror filled her for a split second. Then, her chest heaved, and she took a huge, gasping breath.

This is it. I can't give anymore.

She wondered if she could hold him off long enough by herself for her friends to escape.

"Don't give up. You can do this."

For a moment, Maya thought it was her own brain arguing with itself. Then she realized the voice was *outside* her head.

And male.

She spared a quick glance to the side.

"Blake?"

It was he, disheveled hair, tattered clothes, and all. He looked worse than dead, yet still managed a wan smile.

"It's time to end this once and for all."

Then, to her amazement, Stuart nodded at Blake and let go of her hand so Blake could step between them. Icy fingers took hers, and she couldn't believe it as he and Stuart clasped hands.

A jolt of power surged through her, stronger than anything she'd felt from the others. More than love, more than adoration, more than tenacity, it was...

Righteousness.

For over a hundred years, Blake, nothing but a simple stowaway when the Black Lady set sail, had devoted himself to making sure Gavin didn't accomplish his evil task. Like his ancestors before him, he'd risked his life, and possible eternal damnation and torture if he failed. He hadn't done it for personal gain, or publicity, or any other selfish reason.

He'd done it because it was *right*. Because the evil living inside Gavin Hamlin needed to be stopped. She felt it in every muscle, every bone, every fiber of her being. The power of pure, unadulterated goodness.

The one thing they'd lacked.

Maya surprised herself by laughing out loud. "To hell with you, Gavin Hamlin! Eat shit and die!"

She reached deep inside, pulling every ounce of power from every fiber of her being. Hot and cold energies fused inside her, creating something greater than their parts. She focused her eyes on Gavin's chest. Just like Master Spiegel had told her, she pictured a spot not on the target itself, but rather a point a few inches behind her target.

"Pretend there is nothing at all between your hand and the impact point."

She imagined Gavin's body as that of a ghost still, with no more substance than a cloud.

And she struck.

As she'd been taught, she never took her eyes off her target, not even when the neon-pink energy bolt shot out from her and struck Gavin dead center in his chest. Behind him, the glowing oval shattered into radiant darts of light, and the blackness within began to shrink in size. Inside it, the sea-demons' mouths opened in silent cries of frustration as they saw their portal disintegrating.

"Nooo--" Gavin's cry ended in mid-scream, and he dropped the book as several green, scaly tentacles burst free from the gateway and wrapped around his body. He struggled against them, holding out his hands to the watching humans, unable to call for help because of the thick appendage encircling his neck. Maya gasped at the size of it, understanding for the first time that the creatures beyond the gate were much larger than they'd appeared to be. In fact, they were gigantic.

The tentacles lifted Gavin in the air, and then the strangest thing in a night of strangeness happened. They turned Gavin's body sideways and pulled from both ends. Maya raised her arms, afraid she'd be splattered with blood and guts when he got torn in half.

Instead, they pulled something out of him, a ghostly image of Gavin Hamlin, identical to his human body, and retreated back into the dark void with the twisting, fighting shape. A second later, the dark oval shrank down to nothing and disappeared, leaving Gavin's lifeless form on the floor.

For a moment, silence filled the room.

Then Maya broke it with an exultant shout.

"We did it!" She let go of Elsa and Blake. With Gavin's defenses shattered, her own power was more than enough to keep the other sailors immobile. She wrapped her arms around Blake and squeezed with all her might, then turned to hug her grandmother.

Just in time to catch her as she collapsed.

"Grandma!"

Elsa looked terrible, her face drawn and pale, her eyes half-closed.

"I'm alright, dear," Elsa said, her voice barely a whisper. "There's not much left to me after all that."

"What can I do?"

"Let me go, child. I can't stay here any longer. It's time for me to go home."

"Grandma, no!" Maya wanted to hold her tighter, but Blake pulled her away.

"She knows what she's doing, Maya. By keeping her here, you're just making it worse."

"Everything will be fine." Elsa's lips curled up in a weak smile. "Take care of yourself. I love you."

"I love you, too, Grandma. I--" She never finished, as Elsa faded away into nothing.

Maya turned to Blake. "Will I ever see her again?"

Before Blake could answer, Stuart and Lucy joined them, hugging her, pounding her back, forcing her to wipe away her tears and put her grief on hold. With all the laughing and shouting, it took her a moment to hear Blake's voice.

"We can't celebrate yet. There's still work to do."

Maya broke away from her friends. "You are so right. I want this over with. How do we do it?"

"Do what?" Stuart asked.

"Kill them," Blake said.

"Kill who?"

"All of them." Blake motioned towards the immobilized sailors.

"Hell, yeah." Lucy flipped her middle finger towards Gavin's lifeless body. "Send 'em right back to the bottom of the ocean."

Blake ignored Lucy and continued talking. Maya gave him mental points for that. *He's learning.*

"Maya's power has them helpless for now. But they are still alive and dangerous. We have to kill them all, starting with Gavin."

"Gavin? But he's already dead." Lucy's voice was full of surety, which Blake's next words shot to pieces.

"No, he's not. The demons took his spirit, his soul, back to wherever they dwell. But his body was human, remember? It still lives, although it is empty. For now."

"For now?" Stuart asked. "What's that mean?"

"It means another spirit - any spirit, good or bad - can fill it and bring it back to life. It could even be Gavin himself. We cannot take that chance. The next one could be even worse, and we would be at a disadvantage."

Maya nodded. Her struggle had weakened her, she could feel it. If they had to go through something like that again, there'd be no chance of winning.

"Dude, they're ghosts." Stuart frowned. "You can't just kill a ghost."

"They're not ghosts anymore," Maya said, and she knew exactly what Stuart was feeling as his eyes went wide.

"You're talking about--"

"No," Blake interrupted. "It's not murder. They're alive, but they're also not really human. Maya's blood...it made them something more. They cannot die of disease or old age. In fact, they could live forever, unless..."

"Jesus." Stuart bit his lip. "I didn't know...I don't think I can..."

"You don't have to." Maya put her hands on his shoulders. Although she no longer felt attracted to him, she was proud to have him as a friend. He'd come through in the end when it mattered most. "You and Lucy take care of Curtis and Gary. And think of a story to tell the police when we call them."

Turning to Blake, she said, "Show me what to do."

He picked up a jagged piece of wood from the floor. Without saying anything, he walked over to the grizzled old sailor who'd tried to kill her.

And stabbed the wood into the sailor's chest.

Like a scene from a vampire movie, Anton Child's body exploded into gray ash.

"Wicked!" Lucy said from where she was kneeling by Gary.

Blake grinned. "That felt good. I always hated him."

He stabbed the next sailor in line, who also turned to dust.

"My turn," Maya said. She went over to Gavin and picked up the knife he'd planned on using to kill her as part of his ceremony. Put her face close to his.

"I hope you rot in Hell." She raised the knife.

And gasped as his eyes opened.

Maya let out a startled cry as his anger reached her through the energy suddenly connecting them again. It was nowhere near as strong as his former power, which was the only thing that saved her. Still, she felt him pushing against her mental defenses, fighting to break through and take over.

"No!" Gripping the knife with both hands, she thrust it into his chest. "This time you die for real!"

Nothing happened.

She pushed harder, but instead of disappearing, he sat up and grabbed her throat with both hands. Dark liquids poured over his lips like a deadly waterfall.

"Stupid bitch. It's you who will die tonight." His words bubbled through the fluids and vile-smelling droplets hit Maya's face.

"Maya!" Blake's voice sounded far away through the sudden ringing in her ears. She couldn't breathe, couldn't scream. Black spots formed before her eyes, and she gripped the knife tighter, twisted it around, and pushed again.

"Gaah!" Gavin let go of her and fell back, thick, black goo oozing from around the knife that stuck out of his chest.

He reached for Maya again, and this time she was the one frozen, held immobile by shock.

He's going to win. I screwed up. I--

Inches from her neck, his arms crumbled into powder.

His screams faded away as the rest of his body disintegrated. Even after he was gone, his cry echoed in Maya's head.

She wondered if she'd hear it forever.

"Are you all right?" Blake turned her around, his face a mix of worry and relief.

"I'm...I'm fine." Each raspy word hurt like hell.

"Go sit down," he said. "I'll finish them."

"Are you sure?"

He smiled. "It will be my pleasure."

Maya nodded her thanks, not wanting to speak anymore. She sat down on the floor and watched as Lucy and Stuart tended to their unconscious friends.

I hope they're okay. God, I'm so tired. Maybe I should close my eyes...

She let her eyelids droop. It felt good. So good...

She didn't open them again for two days.

Chapter 25

When the doorbell rang, Maya ignored it, sure it was more reporters wanting interviews. She'd already seen her face in the papers more than enough, thank you very much. All she wanted to do was enjoy some alone time now that her parents had finally left the house.

"Open the damn door, you silly biyatch. We come bearing munchies and gossip!"

"Lucy!" Maya ran for the door. How had she known to come over?

"We saw your parents' car pull out, so we grabbed snacks and hauled ass back here," Lucy said, as she and Stuart came inside.

"You've been watching my house?"

"Hell, yeah! How else could we know when to come over without fear of prying parental ears?"

"How long do we have?" Stuart asked.

"A few hours. God, I can't believe they're finally gone." Maya let herself sink into the thick cushions of the couch and sighed.

Lucy opened a soda and plopped down in a chair. "Ain't nothing fun about house arrest, that's for sure."

House arrest. Leave it to Lucy to find the perfect term for it. The last three days had been agonizingly boring. Although the doctors had assured everyone the only thing Maya suffered from was exhaustion, they'd also suggested she rest for a couple of days after leaving the hospital. Maya's parents had taken that to mean no leaving the house and no visitors for more than ten minutes at a time. And to make sure she followed the rules, they'd closed the diner and stayed home with her. They'd even taken away computer privileges and monitored her cell phone use, only allowing a few minutes at a time.

By the second day, she'd had enough. Fighting for her life against a century-old ghost and preventing the gates of Hell from opening almost seemed preferable to enduring another round of gin rummy at the kitchen table or listening to her mother ask her if she needed anything.

Not that she'd been totally cut off from outside communication. She'd managed a few clandestine phone calls and emails and tweets with Lucy and some of her other friends. There'd been two visits from the police and at least a half dozen phone calls from different newspapers, which had been kind of cool.

And, of course, the late night visits from Blake although those hadn't involved much talking.

Just a lot of lip action.

As if on cue, Blake materialized in the kitchen and joined them.

Speak of the Devil.

"Hi, everyone."

"Hey." Lucy swiped her hand through his shirt, and chest, as he walked by. "Don't you ever get tired of wearing the same clothes?"

"I don't have much choice." He gave Maya a short but firm kiss and sat down next to her on the couch. She glanced at Stuart, but his face showed no trace of his former jealousy as he dropped into the love seat across from them.

"So, did the doctor give you the all-clear today?"

Maya smiled to herself. It was nice having him and Blake not throwing fists at each other although it was still weird to see them acting chummy.

Who'd have thought?

"Yeah. Clean bill of health, so the parental units decided it was safe for both of them to go back to work for a few hours."

"That means it's party time!" Lucy said, doing crazy pumping motions in the air with her fists.

"Whatever." As much as she wanted to get out of the house, the last thing Maya felt in the mood for was partying.

"What's wrong?" Blake asked.

"Everything." One of the worst parts about being trapped in the house was that she'd been unable to avoid thinking about everything that had happened. "Fiona's dead because of me. And that other girl. And Mary Ellen."

"No great loss there," Lucy muttered.

"Yes, it is!" Maya surprised herself with the vehemence of her words. She knew Lucy's bravado covered up her own guilt; they'd talked about it more than once over the past few nights. Still, it bothered her to think that people - friends and classmates - were dead because of her. "She was a bitch, but she didn't deserve to die."

"It's not your fault," Blake said, echoing the words Maya had told Lucy the night before. He leaned closer and took her hand. She knew he was right, just like she'd known it the dozen-odd other times he'd told her, lying next to her in the dark of her room the past nights. But knowing something and believing it, *feeling* it, were totally different things. At least for her.

In the end, it didn't matter what anyone said. She still felt responsible.

After all, it'd been her blood Gavin needed, not only to become human again but also to do his freaky spell.

"I don't believe it. You think this all happened because of you?"

Everyone turned and looked at Stuart, whose face had gone red and angry.

"Yes, I do. Without me, none of it would've been possible."

"Really? So it's your fault the Black Lady sank here a hundred years ago? That a psycho warlock happened to be on board? That the museum decided to put on an exhibit?"

"Uh, no..." Maya struggled to get the words out. "Not those things, but--"

"And was it your fault that somehow Gavin and his crazy sailors came back as ghosts?" Lucy chimed in.

"That's not--"

Blake spoke over her objection. "Was it your fault you were born with the power to see ghosts?"

Maya shook her head. "No, but it's my fault Fiona went to the museum. And if I hadn't been here, had this power, Gavin couldn't have ever gotten the stupid book in the first place."

"That's where you're totally wrong." Stuart pointed his finger at her. "In fact, if it wasn't for you, there'd be a lot more people dead. Right, Blake?"

"Yes, it's true."

"Wait a minute." Maya's head was spinning. First Stuart and Blake put aside their differences to help her, and now they were actually agreeing on something? "How is that possible?"

Blake continued talking. "Gavin knew the blood of an ordinary virgin could make him human again, even if it was only for a few minutes. Without you, he would have been forced to kill more girls, over and over, so he could keep taking on his solid form to find the book. Nothing was going to stop him."

Maya started to object again, but Stuart interrupted. "Listen to him, Maya. You know the old saying."

"What? What saying?"

"Always respect your elders."

For a moment, everyone stared at Stuart. Then, Lucy burst out laughing.

"Respect your elders! Hoo! Good one, Stu-man!"

Stuart smiled, and even Blake chuckled.

"Okay, fine. I give up." Maya threw her hands up. Who'd have expected all three of them to join forces against her? "It wasn't my fault. Happy now?"

"Yes." Lucy chugged her soda and let out a very Lucy-like belch. "You're a hero. We all are. So besides mourning those we lost, we should be out enjoying our heroic status."

"I still can't believe the police bought your story." Maya'd been unconscious when the police arrived, and so she hadn't had the chance to hear Stuart and Lucy spin their tale of a gang who'd ransacked the Black Lady exhibit for a rare medallion hidden in a box, and then taken off when they found it. When asked about the kidnappings and murders, they'd shrugged and said they had no idea why the men did it.

"They were crazy, talking about spells and the Devil and sacrifices."

When pressed for details, both of them said they'd been hit on the head pretty hard and couldn't remember anything more about what had happened. And because they'd been unconscious the entire time, neither Gary nor Curtis could provide any information that would refute Lucy and Stuart's story. When informed of all this, Maya'd thought it was the most ridiculously outrageous tale she'd ever heard.

The police swallowed it hook, line, and impossible sinker.

The next day, every paper up and down the coast carried the news. "Witchcraft Returns to New England!" "Crazed Gunmen Hold High School Students Hostage!" "Heroic Teens Survive Museum Massacre!"

"Hurray for small town police," Lucy said, digging into a bag of pretzels. Crumbs sprayed out as she spoke. "For once it pays off."

"How is your grandmother?" Blake asked, not-so-subtly changing the subject. Maya smiled at him, showing her appreciation for his tactics. Besides, it was nice to have some good news.

"Fine, after some much-needed rest. She said she's gonna have to check up on me more often, to make sure I'm staying out of trouble."

"It still weirds me out," Stuart said.

"What? That my dead grandmother talks to me?"

"No, I kind of expect that sort of weirdness from you. Actually, I'd expect it from Lucy first, but you're a close second."

Lucy snorted, spraying more pretzel crumbs on Stuart's arm. "This coming from a guy who gets his rocks off doing long-horn sheep imitations while trying to capture a piece of inflated leather."

"Eat another pretzel, Lucy," Maya said. "So what's bothering you, Stuart?"

"That ghosts exist at all. No offense, Blake, I mean, you seem like a decent guy and all, but if ghosts exist, what other things are real?"

"Well, we know demons are real." Maya crossed her arms and hugged herself as a shiver ran through her. Just the thought of those creatures...

I'm gonna have nightmares about them for a long time. Thanks a lot, Gavin Hamlin. That's another one I owe you for.

"From the things Gavin spoke about, I have a feeling there were many more unpleasant surprises in that book."

Stuart frowned. "Speaking of the book, where is it?"

"Yeah," Lucy said. "The last thing we need is someone else getting their hands on it. That thing should be put through a shredder and then burned."

"Gone." Blake shrugged. "I went back and looked as soon as I knew Maya was alright."

"It must have exploded when Gavin died," Stuart said. "Or maybe he took it with him to Hell or wherever he is."

"Good riddance." Lucy belched again.

Maya glanced at Blake, saw the same consternation in his gaze that she felt. They'd talked about it already. Both of them remembered seeing Gavin drop the book.

Before the tentacles came and grabbed him.

It was possible the book disintegrated, its magical existence tied to its owner.

Possible, yes. But Maya didn't believe it.

Somehow, I don't think we've seen the last of that thing.

Blake patted her hand, letting her know his thoughts mirrored hers. Out loud, though, he changed the subject once again.

"Maya, what time are your parents coming home?"

She grimaced. "Tonight? I doubt they'll work late. Probably rush right home after the dinner crowd to make sure their fragile little flower is still alive. Why?"

"That gives us almost three hours," he said.

"For what?" Maya's confusion only grew stronger when Lucy and Stuart started laughing.

"C'mon, Stu-man, that's our cue. We're outta here." Lucy pointed at Maya. "Tomorrow night, oh clueless one. Bowling. Boys. Berry wine coolers. I don't care if we have to lock your parents in the basement. We're celebrating. Our legions of admirers expect it of us, and we need to take advantage of it before we're yesterday's news."

She grabbed a still-chuckling Stuart and led him out the door.

Maya turned to Blake. "What are they talking about?"

Two seconds later, Maya's confusion disappeared as Blake's lips against hers explained everything.

It was the best celebration she could have asked for.

CPSIA information can be obtained at www.ICGtesting.com
263390BV00002B/4/P

9 781936 564095